Dragons Cry

Also by Tessa McWatt:

Out of My Skin (1998)
ISBN 1-896332-08-0

Dragons Cry <small>a novel</small>
Tessa McWatt

The Riverbank Press

Cover and text design: John Terauds
Cover illustration: *Longing* by Pamela Williams, used with permission

THE CANADA COUNCIL | LE CONSEIL DES ARTS
FOR THE ARTS | DU CANADA
SINCE 1957 | DEPUIS 1957

We acknowledge the support of The Canada Council for the Arts for our publishing program.

Canadian Cataloguing in Publication Data

McWatt, Tessa
  Dragons cry

ISBN 1-896332-13-7

I. Title.

PS8575.W37D72 2000   C813'.54   C00-930939-X
PR9199.3.M38D72 2000

The Riverbank Press
P.O. Box 456, 31 Adelaide St. East, Toronto, Ontario, Canada M5C 2J5

Printed and bound in Canada by Transcontinental Printing

For Tony

Acknowledgements:

Many books assisted me in the development of this novel; in particular, *Mozart*, Wolfgang Hildesheimer, translated from the German by Marion Faber (J.M. Dent and Sons, Ltd., London, 1982); *A–Z of Barbadian Heritage,* Fraser, Carrington, Forde, Gilmore (Heinemann Publishers Caribbean Ltd., Jamaica, 1990); *The Time Before History*, Colin Tudge (Touchstone, New York, 1996); *Mapping it Out*, Mark Monmonier (Chicago: University of Chicago Press, 1993); *Neptune's Gift*, Robert P. Multhauf (John Hopkins University Press, Baltimore and London, 1978); and the King James Bible.

Excerpts from the following song lyrics are quoted in the novel: "When a Man Loves a Woman," by Percy Sledge; "A Case of You," by Joni Mitchell; "Lizard," by Mighty Sparrow; "Wild is the Wind," by Nina Simone; "Like a Rolling Stone" and "I Shall Be Released," by Bob Dylan; "What's Going On," "I Want You," and "Mercy Mercy Me (The Ecology)," by Marvin Gaye.

I am grateful to Errol McWatt, Gregory McWatt, Jackie Kaiser, Fides Krucker, Susan Shipton, Mary Shipton, Anna Tchernakova, Lynne Cohen, Andrew Lugg, David Clemis, and Stephanie Young for their contributions to the development of this novel. Heartfelt thanks to Attila Berki for guidance and careful editing. I'm grateful for the generous hospitality and inspiration of my friends in The Garden, Christ Church, Barbados: Margaret and Keith Walcott, Margot and Nat Clairmonte, Christopher Skinner, and Dorothy Skinner. Special thanks to my friends Frederick Clairmonte and Sean Carrington.

The author gratefully acknowledges the Ontario Arts Council for its support.

ONTARIO ARTS COUNCIL
CONSEIL DES ARTS DE L'ONTARIO

Until this day, nobody has seen the trekking birds take their way toward such warmer spheres as do not exist, or the rivers break their course through rocks and plains to run into an ocean which is not to be found. For God does not create a longing or a hope without having a fulfilling reality ready for them. But our longing is our pledge, and blessed are the homesick, for they shall come home.

— Isak Dinesen, *Anecdotes of Destiny*

CHAPTER 1

Salt

"Mercy," she said, with a gurgle like grinding pearls from the back of her throat. "Mercy, Mercy me," when she spotted the broken shards of porcelain scattered in the driveway. Then MacKenzie sucked her teeth in a "*s-t-c-h-u-p*" and pivoted toward the house. Warning enough for Simon who heard in that *stchup* the decree of the lash that would lick his backside when his father got home.

On the heals of mercy came music from the back room of the house as Simon's brother cranked up the volume on the record player. By the time MacKenzie returned from the house with a broom and dustpan, the singer was belting out the melody with a leathery hunger in his voice. The man who sang all day long, "*when a man loves a woman . . . can't keep his mind on nothin' else . . . he'd trade the world for the good thing he's got,*" was lashing Simon's heart. The whole neighbourhood sang along, as though the singer was in their gardens and not compressed on a flat black disc. Simon's brother had bought the record a week before and was wearing it out.

When she's bad he can't see it . . . she can do no wrong . . .

MacKenzie grimaced and cupped her ears for a second before stooping to sweep up the remnants of the vase which, until just a few minutes earlier, had sat empty near the entrance to the house. Placed there four years earlier in an unribboned moment of welcome to the island by his mother's cousins, the vase and its future as an heirloom were shattered. MacKenzie picked up a slice of the porcelain on which a fair, dainty woman in bonnet and flowing dress dipped her ruffled turquoise parasol as she stepped up to a waiting carriage. The servant looked up and cut her eyes spitefully at Simon, who ran behind the house, dragging his cricket bat.

Simon had toppled the vase during an otherwise perfect, full-arched swing of his bat, which would have sent them to their feet at the cricket oval, he was sure. He had been practising all afternoon in the shade of the carport, swinging for fictive cheers. His swing was improving daily.

But MacKenzie didn't understand cricket. She didn't understand the whole Carter family, nor trust their Guyanese continentalism. From the moment the Carters had moved to Barbados from Guyana, they'd had nothing but bad luck with the housekeeping servants they'd taken on, and there'd been many who'd decided to leave before the first week was out. Shining sable-skinned women had stared at the four Carter children and had shaken their heads or raised their hands with the *Hallelujah* or *Lord I am a witness* flailings of a revival meeting. But MacKenzie had stayed, persevered, as though chosen by her god.

One day, she'd lined up the four children in order of age and height and bent down to stare each in the eye, incredulous that the four had come from the same parents. Faces of chaos, not one of them resembling the other. Two foreheads were wide bands of copper skin over gentle bumps of bone. The skin was framed in one case by straight black hair, and in the other by biscuit-coloured ringlets. In the third child, the cheekbones were high like the side of a dry valley, the almond-shaped eyes tapering off into the ridges of bone. The fourth child, with natty hair, had the same wide forehead, but the skin was coffee-coloured and pocked with adolescence. Noses: two pugged and flat, one wide and bridged, and the fourth barely making its presence known between chubby cheeks. And eyes: dark except for one pair of shimmering shamrock green. Like a box of assorted sweets, the multiformity was dazzling, and MacKenzie gulped back an anxious hiccup, vowing then and there to do her duty and not be tempted into speculating about God's purpose.

Trust was a winding train for both family and housekeeper, gathering speed throughout the years and arriving, finally, today at Simon's brother's funeral. But on that August afternoon, with Simon swinging awkwardly into puberty, the tension was high. As MacKenzie strained her broad, refrigerator back to sweep up his gallant gaffe, Simon peeked at her from around the corner of the house and watched the crease of the cotton shift enter the crack between her immense buttocks. His boyhood creaked arthritically. Then, from the window, more singers, female voices in unison, joined in the singing, accompanying the man who loved a woman, *ooo oh, ooo oh—try to hold on to the love we knew, crying baby, baby, please don't do me wrooooong—ooh*. The neighbourhood moaned, rolling over on itself.

Death always brings that memory. At every funeral Simon has attended in the decades since he broke the vase, that moment replays itself in his mind's eye. Today was no exception. He worries that he may even have let slip a grin as his mother threw the first handful of earth over the coffin, and that perhaps from the other side of the grave Faye saw it flicker across his face. If she did, she hasn't let on. But what if she misconstrued it? It had been the wind's fault. The wind blew up near the end of the ceremony and the women's hats looked as though they would fly off. But something, a certain requirement of dignity, kept them in place. It must have been that certain requirement that forced the memory—always does. The dignity of a stoop.

It was the police chief's hat that finally held Simon's gaze. The black brim was pulled down over the man's brow, hiding the eyes but not the occasional quiver of the mouth. Simon watched him with teetering sentiments, knowing only parts of the story and the pointed fingers of blame, but he eventually gave in to pity as he watched a tear run down the cheek before being brusquely wiped away.

But the other elements of the childhood memory—the heat, the music—clash with today's indecencies of hymns and wailing, the patting of displaced earth, and the wreath of rust and yellow leaves David's children arranged beside the grave. David used to love October: the changing colours, the dying light. He said it was the month that kept him in Canada, the one time of year he could feel angels around him. Simon never understood that about his brother, along with so much else. His own response to autumn is simple: it drives thoughts deeper into his head and his testicles up into his belly. He remains curled up on himself until April. But it's these autumn ruminations that he must now, tonight, unfurl—straighten like a steamed collar, press hard on the wrinkles in his brother's life, and flatten a path toward tomorrow . . . and Faye.

Simon's feet are numb from the cold. He reaches down to his left foot. The compass bulges in his right-hand pocket. He peels back his sock and touches the skin: like refrigerated meat, dead meat . . . like his brother.

Is he cold? The earth is beginning to freeze around him, to preserve him until next spring when rain will soak his coffin and leak onto the satin, staining it like tears on a pillow. *The concentration of salt in a tear is higher than in the ocean. The stain is deeper. High salt concentrations are bacteriostatic, but can be washed away by water. Salt of the earth.*

In Barbados, MacKenzie used to tell Simon that God would accept only sacrifices that were salted. "Every oblation that you offer, you must never fail to put on your oblation the salt of the covenant with your God," she quoted the Old Testament. "You are the salt of the earth." She salted their food and sugared their tea beyond all recognition, and he wonders now if his lifelong fascination with salt was spawned through food—a quest to reconcile the inside and the outside, guts and earth.

Simon rubs his toes. He thinks he can hear Faye upstairs in her studio. She isn't practising, but she might be studying her part because there is a loud thumping of a heel, a tapping out of rhythm. They have been separated by a storey since arriving home from the funeral. Without a word, each drifted to the extremities of the tiny house, Faye to her studio, Simon to his desk in the basement. *I think it's a fugue she's learning, isn't that what she told me?—I can't keep the forms straight.* She's always working these days, playing the cello all the time and so full of notes that they pop out of her mouth at the dinner table between chews. A week ago she blurted out *ta dee dee ta* in a green spew of spinach. She giggled, almost ashamed of being so happy. Simon had noticed a returning sparkle in her bright green eyes, the creeping flush on her creamy cheeks. Until all this happened. *I shouldn't stay down here too long or she'll accuse me of hiding feelings from her.*

Nannerl. Mozart's sister. She keeps hopping into Faye's thoughts, as though in a game of skipping, finding Nannerl in the middle, between the beating ropes of all that is going on around her. How in tandem ran the lives of Nannerl and Wolfgang until that age when girls became women and boys went on to be geniuses. The Mozart children played together like a circus act, travelling through Europe performing four-handed music for anyone who paid the entrance fee to the cashier, their father, Leopold. It's said that Leopold heaved huge sighs of frustration when a prince, having deigned to hear the Mozart children play, rewarded them merely with praise, or a small gift for Nannerl, but nothing for the budding divinity himself. Faye is pursuing a moral in this poetic justice, wondering how talent and fate get either braided or left dangling loose, like fly-away hair. Why did Ms. Nannerl surface today at David's funeral? Skip, skip in time with the piston of fate, then in jumped *unfair*, a word she's been sounding out all afternoon: *fair, fair, unfair, who's the fairest, so unfair*. Is that what made her think of Nannerl? She is still numb with disbelief, refusing to accept that David has killed himself, and she has decided to stay busy, to practise, to think only of music, to think in sounds . . . *damn, damn, damn*. Perhaps the thought of Nannerl was inspired by the rivalry between siblings, or the shadow of unfulfillment, remembering how much David overshadowed his younger brother.

She pushes away words she is incapable of saying to Simon, unable, as she has been all week, to tear open a corner of the tight package of death to allow a conversation to pour out about suicide, about how he might be coping with the suicide of his own brother. She knows she must approach Simon about David, about the envelop she hid in the chest a few days ago, about the shadow that has drawn over her too, and how frightened she is about words she doesn't want to hear. *There's no place like* . . . But she can't. Not yet. *Push, push, push* . . . only sounds.

She pictures Simon in the basement at his desk, pretending to read but staring at bare stucco walls. Instead of going to him, she's hiding up here in her studio pretending to practise and performing the occasional silent arpeggio with her left hand on the cello's neck. *Tap tap tap.*

Faye stares out the window. The last of the leaves are holding feebly onto branches, and the sky is irritated the way she is at this time each month, knowing her body is soon to erupt and flow. The symptoms arrive earlier each month, and even today, a day of ovulation, she feels them: moodiness like glue. *And tonight . . . will we? Could we?*

She has been considering a sort of voodoo for herself,

wondering if she should perform it at the next opportunity. Wary of cures now, she nevertheless found herself fascinated by how this one was prescribed, with the tone of certainty in Simon's mother's voice that seemed to say *I know, I know.* Grace, Edwin, and the rest of the family arrived four days ago from Barbados, and Faye could sense Grace gripping onto the certainty of birth in the way she held tight to her handbag, as though someone would snatch that too away from her. Faye convinced her to sit down to a cup of tea, but still Grace clutched the bag in her lap. Their conversation turned to the children, to David's now fatherless three, and Grace paused before looking up at Faye to say firmly, "Make haste, enough waitin' now. You two must make a chile."

It was impossible for Faye to tell her it had been months since she and Simon had brushed skin to skin. Grace became distracted in thoughts that brought a frown, and Faye felt a rush of shame, wondering what Grace was thinking about her as she stared at the tiled floor, a hint of knowledge in her lips.

"An Amerindian woman in Guyana once told me a sure-fire way to get pregnant: After intercourse, ya suck the centre out of a raw egg, slap your belly five times, turn in a circle, then lie with your legs straight in the air for an hour. Works in the most stubborn cases."

Curatives like these have had a way of lodging in Faye's brain since her days at the clinic, but the tone was far too absolute, and she knows that it's more than a stubborn body she must deal with. *Push, push . . . only sounds.*

Hup, four, three, two, one . . .

Many years before Faye met Simon, she and Michael tried to have a child. They made their monthly visits to the fertility clinic, where they call them work-ups as though they were a prelude to an aerobics class—*again, four, three, two, one*—demoralising treatments that made her mood even fiercer than the slate grey clouds she can see approaching from the east.

She's grateful to Simon that he refuses to undergo such "therapy," but she has sensed his recent floundering around science. He who has always relied on reason is now full of contradictions. In the wake of death he is uncharacteristically philosophical, incapable of decoding suicide.

Faye exhales heavily.

Suicide sneaks up, attacks, but doesn't retreat. Instead it lingers to taunt with missed warning signs. No one in David's family expected it, not even his ex-wife, Justine, who'd spoken to him on the telephone that morning. Along with their grief, the family is battling guilt and despair for not having prevented his death. And there was more despair in the tears of the police chief and the sobs of David's fellow guards from the Newmarket jail, who stood confused and awkward in the church.

Simon is coming up the stairs. His gait is as heavy as a workhorse, *clop, clop. Will we touch?*

Simon puts on the sweater that hangs near the front door, then glides into slippers, feeling suddenly caught inside the freeze frame he has of his father: middle-aged, slippered feet propped up on the long mahogany arms of his Berbice chair as he reads *Time Magazine* cover to cover. But his father is an old man now, and Simon feels guilt slithering along his shoulders—the snaky feeling of never being enough has grown heavier. The light-weight things he and his father say to each other these days come out like electrical shocks, and Simon is always surprised by how much he holds back. In letters and phone calls he inquires after health, relatives, changes of government at home, but never what he wants to ask—questions he has yet to frame— and he absorbs his father's electrostatic responses with the grounding *uh huh*s, and *oh dear*s he must have memorized as a child. With the whole family in town, including MacKenzie, it was impossible to have them all stay in their small east-end home, which barely tolerates two. Or was it? He might have done more. Always "might" and "more"—strong and obedient words.

The house is silent. No sounds from Faye's studio, as if it's sealed off. Often at home it feels as though pockets of air separate him from Faye. Bubbles that promise to burst open and allow them to breathe freely and deeply of each other, but never do. He just keeps bumping into them and bouncing away like a stray balloon.

He presses the play button that starts the CDs stacked in the player and walks back downstairs, now delicate in his step. His fine bones are cranky with sleeplessness.

He knows that Faye is being generous, allowing him to bounce away from her, but what he needs now, most of all, is a strong connection to something that will keep his blood flowing in the right direction. Office work doesn't seem to help. Functionaries who cannot function. He sits down at his desk, slides his foot in and out of its slipper, then picks up the assessment data he has been studying.

Functionaries who underfunction. Simon and the other clerks shuffle in each day to their offices on Queen's Park Crescent at the cartography division of the Ontario Ministry of Natural Resources. Here Simon compiles, updates, and catalogues grid maps, surveys, and geological data. Plans for developments and subdivisions are registered with the provincial government, and their impact on the landscape is transferred to the appropriate provincial map. Simon's job involves cross-referencing new maps with their immediate predecessor, the careful monitoring of changing topography. This process winds back to original land surveys done at the time of Lord Simcoe, and Simon finds the process prismatic, with each frame of change on a map refracting whole ways of living we can no longer imagine. Rock has become brick and siding. Land adjusts to its users. *Terra* is not *firma* but rather the gentle accident of time, wind, and machines reshaping sediment and water. Rock changes, Simon knows, but the work of the shuffling functionaries remains the same. He has learned to cross-reference everything, including his own life, ticking off items on a check-list—job, home, relationship—and carefully placing life's shifts in neat grids with clear explanations and symbols. He has been careful not to defy the logic of scale, but David's death does just that.

Some days he would like a good fight, like the ones in the mining camps up north. Men from the rigs, in town for Saturday night with more money in their pockets than he now makes all year, would scramble on top of each other over a look or a word inflected in a code he could never decipher. Trained as a geologist and apprenticed to an oil company to conduct seismic surveys, Simon had been helicoptered into the bush of northern Alberta to listen to the earth. To detect in the belching echo of dynamite the layers of hard or soft sediment that would signal oil. But he soon realised he would not last in the bush, that if he stayed he would become like the other men. In the cartography division he sometimes misses the rumbling of anger that ran through his days in the north. Office battles are stale and futile, but he feels an explosive one coming. Rumours have it that the provincial government will restructure the ministry, bring in new technology that will eliminate half of the jobs. He has been wondering what he will do when this work is gone.

For the moment, he is fixed on erosion, the silent falling away of the Scarborough Bluffs into Lake Ontario. Under pressure from both property owners and conservationists, the ministry has commissioned an assessment of the eroding bluffs, the data for which sits on Simon's desk in the basement. He wasn't chosen as part of the assessment team, but he borrowed the reports and brought photocopies home to try to form his own conclusions. The project of sand, as he calls it to himself.

He fears the government has chosen the malfunctioning functionaries knowing they will write the report it wants, one which details the inordinate cost and impossibility of saving cliffs of sand that will forever drizzle into the lake. "That's nature," his hard-rock geologist colleagues would say, but the conservationists point to over-development, poor drainage, and abnormal weather patterns. Simon senses something has been left out of both arguments, so he has been pursuing the hard data these last few weeks in the basement. Sand as sand, its properties and short-comings—an invisible report that will rescue his reason.

He has been unable to concentrate since long before David's death. At the office, the maple tree that is growing outside his window sheds its leaves, now nearly naked before his day-long stare. Simon taps vigorously on his keyboard and clutches the phone to his ear when anyone comes to his quiet oak office. He wishes he could stare at that brazen maple tree now, here in the basement. But he is alone.

I should go back to salt. Or at least return to science that's firm and grounded, doesn't sift through fingers: In the sea there is a 3.5% solution of salts, of which 2.5% is sodium chloride. Evaporation separates sodium chloride from the water, and from other salts, which constitute over 28% of the saline content of sea water. Of the several salts present in sea water or brine, only sodium chloride is present in sufficient quantity and has the appropriate solubility characteristics to precipitate out before the solution has been reduced to a small fraction of the original. There is sanity and beauty there.

I would like to take her to me tonight, to touch her in a soft spot behind her ear, the spot that makes her dissolve in my hands, but I am frightened.

Bartok slides up into the speakers. The sound a CD makes when it begins makes Faye think of a figure skater gliding up to a bold full stop in the centre of a rink to await her musical cue. She's always wanted to do that: perform a double-bladed parallel stop that sends ice flying.

The string quartet reminds her of Paris, two years ago, with Simon. The airline tickets arrived at work, along with a dozen roses that were meant to tug at the string of forgiveness that dangled between them. The telephone sales office where she works is crowded with operators in cubicles, and they all watched her as she opened the envelope, embarrassed by the extravagance of Simon's gift. The shame around love and telephones re-emerges, but she pushes the reasons away . . . *boing, boing* . . . and tries to skate with Bartok back to the charms of Paris. She and Simon had walked through the streets, always touching, temporarily released from the reasons for the trip.

For Faye, Paris was a latchstring to herself. She had lived there for six months just after university, believing that to be a real artist one had to be in Paris, as if inspiration and talent might just rub off the museum walls or be found floating in a café au lait. *Plat, plat* at the braid of fate. But she had walked, lonely and poor, up and down the Champs Elysée like a *femme disparu* looking to belong, daring herself to shout: "*New York Herald Tribune—New York Herald Tribune*"—like the girl in Godard's film. But on her trip with Simon, she delighted in the gaze of cherubs, gargoyles, and sword-bearing angels that watched her from their perches. She saw the Michelangelo statues anew, knowing then that they were imitation Davids; the penises of many had been gashed off by weather and age, but they remained casually reclining, showing her the cracked plaster at their crotches. *Ouch.*

She and Simon visited Père Lachaise, the resting place of Balzac, Molière, Colette, Jim Morrison, and so many others. It was the one place in the city she felt Simon relax, as if in death he could find himself inside the culture, one corpse not surpassing the carbon quality of any other. They strolled through the cobblestone streets of that city of the dead, following maps and signs marking elfin avenues to the tombs. Rows and rows of mausoleums, like miniature chateaux, were engraved with names—Famille Crépon, Famille Hermand. Generations turning to dust together. Walking among the broken monuments and weedy stone, they talked about burial and faith. Unlike Simon, Faye had not been baptised—another sliver of her history that surprised him.

"You never mentioned that before."

"Not important, really." She could see Simon getting uncomfortable. "My parents didn't believe in it, were never much for ceremonies. Quietly atheist, I suppose."

Simon was visibly disconcerted. Faye went on, half mollifying, half teasing, "Of course, our children will be christened." She paused, waiting for his agreement, then couldn't stop herself from joking, "like taking out an insurance policy on their souls." She looked at him anxiously. Simon nodded seriously and said, "Yes, good, that would be best," and even that hint of a future between them made Faye walk more confidently. There was hope in the cracks of every tombstone they examined. Finally, had death released them from the past? *And now? No, push, push, remember just the charms . . .*

She remembers the heat from Simon's face. On the third day of their holiday, his fever was so intense he couldn't get out of bed, but insisted she go out and enjoy herself. She set off on a shopping spree on Rue de Rivoli. In the metro her eyes caught a flash of blue and green, and a face she suddenly recognised. The woman had been the concierge in the building where Faye had once rented a tiny *chambre de bonne*. Her face was the one Faye had spied every day behind the lace curtains of her always slightly ajar door. Madame Letellier would sit in a Louis XIV-styled chair watching what little coming and going there had been in the foyer—a blank stare surveying all that might have been, given another life, another age. She was a fixture, a daily apparition, and a reproduction of the hundreds of other diminutive French women Faye had seen sitting endlessly staring out from behind veils of tarnished lace. Amazingly, she now thinks, Madame Letellier recognised her.

"Est-ce-que c'est vous? La Canadienne?"

"Oh Madame, oui. Comment-allez-vous?"

"Ça va, ça va," the old woman said wearily.

Madame Letellier's appearance was startling. She was petite and had the most fancifully decorated eyes Faye had ever seen—lime green mascara and turquoise lids. And there they were across the aisle in the metro, looking the same as they had so many years ago through the crack of her door, if only just slightly more wrinkled, and consequently more decorated.

"Are you still always in the *salle de concert*?" Madame Letellier asked, practising her English.

Something punched Faye under the ribs. "No, not recently," she answered, sensing the deep hole she'd carved for herself by having banished music when she'd abandoned Michael. "I'm here just for a week," she added. Excuses, excuses.

Madame Letellier blinked, "Mais . . ."

Faye knew that the woman remembered her as the auburn-haired music student who couldn't stay out of a concert hall. But since those hopefully breathless days of Paris when she was twenty-two, music had seized her, devoured her, then spit her out.

"I invite you at my home . . . to play . . . *et on prendra un coup ensemble . . .*"

Pianissimo. Until that moment, Faye had not given words to her abandonment of music. She had just stopped, become silent.

"I think I've forgotten . . . how . . ." she mumbled to Madame, whose peacock eyes fanned her with incomprehension. The train arrived at Chatelet. Before Faye got off, she kissed the woman on both cheeks and felt the lashes tickle the side of her face. She emerged onto the street in front of the Chatelet Theatre. Walking past it on her way to Rivoli, she caught sight of a poster listing that night's performance—Bartok's string quartets performed by the Tokyo Quartet. *Crash*. Bartok's string quartets had been the last music she'd learned and never performed. It was automatic; she found herself at the ticket window buying two places for that night.

She convinced Simon to get out of bed to accompany her, but their seats were up in the heavens, which must have increased the pressure in his sinuses, adding to his misery. She sat nervously awaiting the first chord. On its arrival, something broke through; a gush of fertile tears. She peeked over at Simon who seemed confounded, but, she believes, a few seconds later he must have understood the significance of this moment, because he took her hand, put it to his cheek, and held it there. His feverish skin warmed her, and she entered his deep, laboured breaths, melting into him. She started to feel drunk, and half-way through the andante of the fifth quartet other music entered her head: a pop song she used to listen to when she'd first met Simon. *I could drink a case of you, and still be on my feet, oh I would still be on my feet.* Music of two worlds playing a duet in her head. She could claim both now. When she and Simon returned to Toronto, she bought a new cello and started playing again, just on and off, the way a person who has reached a point of near starvation has to eat only small morsels over long periods to prevent the system from going into shock. Eventually, all the music became hers again, thanks to Bela Bartok and some green mascara on a funny little woman in the metro.

Tonight the violins in the swelling second quartet are like whitecaps and the house is being heaved about by eighth notes. The crescendo makes death feel small.

Bartok travels to the basement.

The first classical music concert Simon ever went to was
with Faye in Paris. He remembers being sick and sleepy and
that the first movement was a soft, enveloping blanket. He
remembers reaching for Faye's hand, just before drifting off, to
touch it to his cheek, offering his fever as an excuse for being
disconnected from an event she wanted to share with him. She
accepted. When he woke for the final movement, he had the
sensation of jumping up high in an effort to reach some
unspecified mark, to understand the sounds, only to hit a barrier
as visceral as a physical blow. He wanted to go home.

Where he was from classical music was what you heard in
church. No one he knew listened to it just for pleasure, and
even in church it was a hybrid form—hymns played on an
organ with a syncopated bass beat. Music had immigrated to
Barbados in the same way as had the Carter family. Calypso
from Trinidad, reggae from Jamaica, and soul music from
Motown. Simon's family, via David, consumed it all. The music
they listened to was "black"—black people's music. David
would bring home albums and style himself after the men
shown on the covers, wearing an unwilling Afro and calling
himself "black" even before everyone else was told they weren't
"coloured" anymore.

His skin was the darkest of all of the children in the family;
he most closely resembled his great great grandfather, a heavy
set Mulatto whose mother had been a slave on a plantation in
the Corentyne region of Guyana. As the eldest, David pushed
limits, extended family boundaries—the first to drive, the first
to come home "stinkin' drunk," the first to defy his father's
whip—and Simon and his sisters had to choose between following his exaggerated lead or protecting the family from his

unpredictability. Francie adored her big brother, and only she could occasionally sway David from provoking his parents. As the younger brother, sometimes ignored, more often bullied because of his quiet, tractable nature, Simon was especially susceptible to David's ganglord rule.

As a result, the only music that really meant anything to Simon was Motown. Smokey Robinson, The Temptations, Marvin Gaye. That was music. Faye's world, so controlled and structured, was peculiar. She moved to pinched sounds that fell into straight lines. When he met her he tried to move to her music, but found it inaccessible, just as there's a part of her he sometimes can't find; even now, Bartok's siren strings are not pulling, but rather pushing him away from her, from today and the funeral.

Simon gets up and goes to the far corner of the basement to where a newly finished pine bookshelf is standing. It's a little off-kilter despite all the care he took, and he can't figure out why. The bookcase was built over two weeks ago. A place for Faye to shelve her thoughts, to store her musical scores. He wanted to finish it sooner, the first gift he's been able to offer her for such a long time, to approach her, if only just in wood. But too much work, then David, and now his will is thirsty and receding. He runs his finger along the scrollwork on the top shelf. The wood is rough. As he searches for sandpaper, the music pushes him into the past.

That day in August—the day he broke the vase—Percy Sledge was the man who loved a woman and could keep his mind on nothin' else. David and his friends were the same. They were upstairs in David's room gawking at naked women in magazines, laughing, hanging out—liming. Every afternoon, David was on the phone to the boys: "Why y'all don' come lime by me nuh?" and in no time at all Stretch, Frankie, and Nat would strut up the driveway and stride right past MacKenzie, without so much as a word to the rest of the family. Mackenzie would seethe beneath her helmet of pot-scrub-brush hair, "Laud, give-she faith!"

The mocking look the boys gave Simon as they passed sent a rush to his groin that made his fingers curl in a ready fist. His eyes dipped to the cement and his breathing warped. He swung his bat hard, hard, again, again, his wild swings the only exaggerated movements in the neighbourhood that day.

That afternoon the air was stifling, barely a whiff of sea breeze blowing into the neighbourhood. Green lizards hid under the veranda rather than perching upside down on the ceiling as they did on days when the breeze was cool. The noisy whistling night frogs dozed under rocks in the flower bed where the hibiscus and bird of paradise drooped, forbearing in these last days before the rainy season.

Simon's older sister, France, named for a trip his mother never took, lay in a hammock under the breadfruit tree reading romance fiction. She was always reading romance. "Francie, Francie, give me some romancie ..." David's friends would chant at her, cupping their hands to their own breasts, squeezing them and holding them out for a nibble. A single dart of Francie's sharp slanted eyes would slice off their stares, gelding their lust, then she'd waddle away to find her place in the shade to read.

Francie's features were the most startling in the family: her mother's Chinese mother sideswiped her father's Amerindian grandmother, leaving her face mashed yet ample, with jiggery smiles. In a long line of rugged females, Francie was a fragile and dreamy anomaly. Unlike her female ancestors, she was tall and broad in the hips in a way that made her legs disappear. A demure, squat-faced deer, she traipsed through the Garden looking for love. Boys found themselves stuck to her oozy allure.

Adored from afar by boys and men in the neighbourhood, Francie was the desired yield of the gardener's working days.

From time to time, Best, who would peer over ferns to watch Francie as she read in her hammock, would draw her cryptic emblems of love on the back of Ting softdrink labels, fold and sail them over a shrub to land at her feet. On one occasion, after Francie had vacated her hammock, Simon watched Best stoop to pick up the book she had left behind and flip its pages, sizing up his competition. Some expected Best to ask Francie to marry him, though she was then just fifteen to his almost thirty years, but Francie would never have considered such an offer from someone who in no way resembled the great heroes of her romance novels: men with names like Lance and Wesley—nothing as clearly overstated as Best. But the neighbourhood gossips didn't pay much attention to Francie's desires. *When a man loves a woman.*

Simon's younger sister Margaret—Maggie—then seven years old, was the one in love with Best. She would follow him around the garden holding up the hose, gallantly trying to ease his burden in the hot sun. In doing so, Maggie would often get too much sun herself and would have to be put to bed before dinner with a fever. But in her fledgling imagination, it was the fever of love, and she looked forward to more days of swooning. Maggie's looks were puzzling. No one in the family knew of ancestors with green eyes or kinky, biscuit-coloured hair and fair skin. In Guyana, the men used to joke with Simon's father that Maggie's looks were the consequence of staying out of town too long on visits to Berbice; others used to tell tales of white jumbies impregnating women in the market; while others smiled the silent smile of the ages, their shining white teeth parting lips like spice ships carving the sea.

Simon's looks fell somewhere between that of the others—a rich muddy blend—which was somewhat of a balm to MacKenzie. He thinks of her now, picturing her face at the funeral, hearing her sing in the chapel, watching the tears polish her face to glazed tar.

He smothers the present, breathes in the Garden.

After moving to Barbados, the Carters settled in the Garden, a neighbourhood in Christ Church named after the original sugar plantation that had spread over the land like a verdant quilt, and had been handed down through generations until the Depression when it was sold and then divided into large properties, then smaller ones, and eventually the residential subdivision known as Garden Gap. The houses there all had names, not numbers, and the Carter house, which had been built on the site of the original boiling house for cane, was called Willowdale. It may have been for that reason alone that Simon chose his first apartment in Toronto in the suburb of the same name.

In Barbados, tell anyone that you were from the Garden and they knew where it was, that like its name it was splendid with foliage and lawns that had been manicured over the razed cane fields. Much of the plantation's original orchards of tamarind, soursop, seagrape, guava, lime, golden apple, and avocado still stood tall when the Carters moved to the Garden, but, as Simon quickly learned, some of them were known by different names in Guyana, and he resented having to call guenips ackees and five finger fruit carambola because the Bajans said it was so. With breadfruit, mango, coconut palm, fern, and pulsating names to dance your tongue over like hibiscus, bougainvillaea, and frangipani, the Garden was bounteous. And like on other islands in the region, the tree of life grew there. But the tree of life in this Garden had not gone wild; it was trimmed and managed with the tenderness that characterised Best's work.

Best came from the country every morning to prune, water, and feed the Garden. He was a tall skinny man with spidery limbs, who to this day has boyish, timeless looks. He and MacKenzie took the same bus in from St. Andrew every morning. Best once told Simon that it was the name of the neighbourhood that had drawn the servant MacKenzie to it in the first place. Paradise. And Best followed. Only when MacKenzie saw the mixed up faces of her charges—"a cook-up family, worse than rice"—did she consider its apostasy.

MacKenzie was a zealot, stern and unwavering in her beliefs. Her evangelism tolerated only purity or complete balance, only what she could interpret using Scripture. Simon was by no means easy, the incident with the vase not being out of character, but compared to the rest, especially David, he was a muddy angel. MacKenzie would tell him stories from the Bible and her own from the country. She said that he was either Simon the Apostle, zealous as fire, second best, or he was Peter, leader of the Apostles, who fished the Sea of Galilee, and who was originally called Simon until the Lord said to him: "Thou art Peter, and upon his rock I will build my church." She preferred the latter interpretation, thinking that one day Simon might be saved and thus transformed. She said: "I know you gon' deny it boy, gon' deny it three times or maybe many more, like he did, but when time comes, you'll be shoutin' his name higher 'n ya natty head and be feedin' he lambs and he sheep." Her fire and brimstone pushed him towards the worship of reason, as he sought shelter from her sermons in his father's practical approach to the world through science. MacKenzie's determination to make him a saint also collided with his own desire to feel like the man in the song who loved a woman to distraction.

Fourteen that August of the broken vase, Simon was obsessed not only with cricket but also with the possibility of his often painful and annoying erection finding a more human deliverance than it had so far experienced. Even at age eleven, in Guyana, he had experimented with ejaculation.

Knox gelatine. Perfect. His instincts had sought out the soft limpid place inside a woman. In their house in the Georgetown neighbourhood of Kitty, on a day when his mother was at the market with Maggie, his father in the country, and neither Francie nor David were at home, he started the careful preparations he had hoped would relieve him once and for all. He retrieved the box of gelatine from the shelf where it sat beside Winston Salt, Quaker Oats Flour, and Lee and Perrins Worcester sauce—their shelf of staples imported from England. The tingle in his penis was like a craving for sweets, and Knox gelatine and dessert had always coincided. Dessert was reserved for parties and would arrive as a dome of orange jelly, dotted with marshmallows. He poured half a box of Knox into a bowl, then followed the instructions to the letter, cooling the gelatine in the freezer for faster result. When it was firm, he placed it in the sun a few minutes to bring it back to a hospitable temperature. By the time it produced a warm, inviting glow, he was ready.

He carried it to the room he shared with David, placed the bowl carefully in the middle of his bed, and barricaded the door with a chair. After stripping, he climbed onto the bed with his jiggling orange companion. A pause while he perched above it, then his eager organ dived in straight, and, with a splat, leaped out again, shocked and shrivelling. The gelatine split apart along a fault-line, slithering and bouncing onto the bed. Defeated, he peeled the mess off the sheets and threw it out the window into the flower bed just as David banged at the door asking why it had been barricaded.

A few months later, he found himself alone in the house again. While rummaging through his father's closet, he came across a condom. He knew that condoms and sex were synonymous, so he took his new treasure into the bathroom, locked the door, unravelled the sheath, and placed it over his now hard penis. He sat on the edge of the bathtub, waiting. Seconds elongated in sync with his blinks. More waiting.

Nothing. He endured endless blinking seconds until the sounds of the keskidee bird's repeated question outside the bathroom window became hypnotising. *Kes kidee? Kes kidee?* Nothing. He had been fooled. Disillusioned, Simon yanked off the condom and flushed it down the toilet. It resurfaced. A twinge of panic. Another flush, but there it floated disobediently. He'd be caught. He waited for the water to refill in the toilet bowl then pressed the handle again, finally sending the latex membrane swirling down the drain.

An organised and efficient man, Simon's father soon noticed his depleted store and confronted David about the missing condom. David's face drooped like a sad dog's, and he looked to Simon, needing for once to be bailed out of a situation not of his own making. Simon avoided his eyes, plunged his hands into the pockets of his shorts, and remained silent. For all the times he'd covered up for David's lies to his parents, hidden the rumours of David's thieving escapades at school, agreed under threat to versions of stories he found difficult to keep consistent, he now did nothing, and felt the moment wage its mute revenge.

Despite his tender eleven years, Simon knew that his older brother had not begun to think about sex. Even before the experiments with the gelatine, Simon had tried to glean some understanding about what was going on with his body, but at his naïve questions David turned quiet. David was humiliated by his father's accusation, not for what it insinuated but for what he had not yet considered. No one suspected Simon. Just the opposite; his girlishness had always been a source of teasing, and not even David thought to accuse him. Instead, that night after dinner, David went into his father's study, where Simon was doing his maths homework, and, as though by way of irrefutable explanation, he held up a single sheet of paper on which he'd written a song. He sang it with a clear, ancient voice. Simon can remember that it began with "Biding my time, necessary waiting," but doesn't recall any other words except the chorus, which rang out with the word "Joy."

Edwin put down his *Time* and listened intently. The *Joy, Joy, Joy* in near falsetto voice rang throughout the room. When David was finished he stood still and blade sharp, waiting for a reaction. Edwin cleared his throat and shuffled the pages of the magazine, looking first at Simon, back at David, and finally fixing his gaze on the bookshelf.

"Well, I think we should all be turning in . . . and you give more thought to what I said earlier."

David disappeared silently into his room.

Simon remembers David, later, in Barbados, in the thick of adolescence, obsession swelling in his neck along veins that striped him with desire. Desire that seemed more than necessary. *Has this all come back to me?*

He feels the sandpaper in his fingers and bends to rub it on the pine. His hand warms as he rubs, and the skin along his forearm feels alight. He slips his foot out of his slipper, folds back the sock and rubs his heel. The music upstairs is softer now. He reaches under the sock to rub his toes with the grainy paper. The skin starts to burn.

Perhaps it was from that incident with the condom that Simon began to track his father's reaction to David.

Edwin and David's attitudes converged on one point: neither could suffer the sermons of MacKenzie. David loudly dismissed her narrowly defined sense of right and wrong, tossing his head like a wild steed as he confronted her views. His father pretended to accept her faith in the eternal and unchanging, quietly undermining her stance with diffident questions that would make Grace secretly smile. The only cross he held to was a Mendelian one of gametes and inheritance. Sentimental in regards to his family—teary to the point of embarrassing his wife on occasion—Edwin viewed his work and much of the world with a dispassionate logic. He held fast to the tenets of science, the gospel of Enlightenment. And, although a veterinarian, he would not tolerate animals to be sentimentalised or anthropomorphised; they were food and for labour, not pets, much to the chagrin of his children.

In Guyana, Edwin had been district supervisor of agriculture, assigned to the eastern province of Berbice. Often he spent weeks away from Georgetown travelling up and down the east coast road performing artificial insemination on local cattle and horses—performances that dropped crumbs on a trail Simon would follow his whole life.

Guyana was toddling toward independence. Agriculture was a primary concern, the key to future stability, and investments were made in cattle stocks, irrigation for rice fields, and sugar mills. Edwin was a consultant on bulls. Venereal disease had plagued the local stocks, and their breeding had resulted in miscarriages and infertility. The tick fever that turned the urine of bulls to blood also transformed the faces of many farmers, who could be found in local rum shops cradling their heads in their hands in despair. But with the introduction of artificial insemination from the finest imported breeds, the country was experiencing an agricultural boom unknown since the height of the sugar trade. The best cattle came from abroad—Brazil, Canada, even India. The imported sires were chosen for their resistance to tropical conditions, primarily heat, and to parasitic infestations. Edwin assisted in the breeding of black-and-white Holsteins, known for their large frame and high milk yield. Smaller brown Jerseys and Guernseys, their butter-fat ratio higher than that of the Holsteins, were bred for the production of cream, butter, and cheese. Diseased beef cattle were eliminated and replaced with hybrids of Brahmans, zebu, and Santa Gertrudis.

For Edwin, nature was dynamic. Heterogeneity was the agenda of living systems: life was fed by all available energies.

He was a mogul of reproduction without copulation, an active participant in a great experiment of mongrelization. The infiltration of exotic breeds increased the likelihood of agricultural success; Guyana would become the force of the continent, he assured his clients. Edwin was a chef, scrambling up gametes, mixing blood, and concocting food for his country with all the hope and anguish of a proud father.

When persistent bellows and continual frustrated mountings indicated that their cattle were in heat, the farmers signalled for Edwin to visit. He was their expert. He led bulls up to a teaser cow, a dummy covered with a convincing soft cowhide. When the bull jumped the teaser, Edwin would grasp its erect penis and lead it into a suitably lubricated rubber sleeve inside a hot-water jacket. The foamy semen collected in a test tube at the end of the sleeve was often enough to impregnate more than one hundred animals—outstripping nature's plodding process.

For inseminations, Edwin's team of technicians first washed the cow's rear with soap and water, grasping the tail and holding it to the side. Then, with his rubber-gloved left hand, Edwin reached into the rectum of the animal, raking out faeces in order to reach the uterus at the cervix. A glass pipet was then inserted into the vagina, and the expanded, in-heat cervix was manipulated over the tip of the pipet with great care. Pressing the syringe at the other end of the pipet, he would express the estimated 1,000,000 sperm found in the 1cc vial of diluted bull semen.

Simon often accompanied his father on day trips to Berbice during the holidays or when he begged long and hard enough to be allowed to skip school. *Daddy, please tek me nuh, Daddy? I don' learn anything in school, and maybe I should be a doctor too.* Appealing to Edwin's acute sense of family usually worked, and along Simon would go on the journey that would bring them home late at night; his mother would find him curled up in the passenger seat, too exhilarated from the day's events to sleep, but exhausted enough to feign slumber in order to be lifted and carried into bed.

The east coast road was a flat, lazily serpentine path connecting the capital to the agricultural heartland. To the right, rice paddies sparkled like breeze-brushed tinsel. To the left lay the sea, flat and brown, stained with jungle silt carried up by the Demerara and Berbice rivers to dirty the coast. This brown water made Simon notorious at school. He had been shocked by the bright cyan of the ocean and sky in Barbados, and the boys in his form, made aware of the muddy coastal waters of his birthplace, used to tease him about being born below sea level, and chant "mudslinging Simon, the simple pie man."

"Man, ya'll could swim in dat brown mess?" they asked. Simon's only retort was one he had learned from David: "Look, we could drag y'all 'hole bloody island down the mouth o' one of we rivers with a steamer, so ya'll watch ya own mouth."

When driving with his father along the east coast road, Simon was put on the lookout for green. It was his responsibility to spot the tell-tale green flags with which farmers signalled that they wanted the vet to stop, either to perform an insemination or to treat a sick animal. White flags for the doctor, green for the vet. The flags were made of anything—green clothes or leaves or branches tied to a stick or a lamppost. Sometimes, his father noted proudly, the farmers had no work for him; they simply flagged him down to share in a celebration, often having slaughtered a sheep for the occasion. Simon took his responsibility seriously and kept a watchful, happy eye out for the various flags. These trips were his early education in applied science, introducing him to the cool glass of the thermometer, the cold steel of the stethoscope, and the warm full vials of the syringes.

On one trip, just after pulling out of a ranch along the road near Fort Wellington, Simon and Edwin were stuck at a crawl

behind a truck carrying a load of cattle headed for market in
New Amsterdam. Edwin checked to his right for oncoming
traffic, pulled out to pass, but ducked back when he saw an
approaching car. Just then a tall, gangly man in a torn shirt and
old straw fedora appeared at the side of the road in front of the
truck. Something flashed. The straw hat flew towards the wind-
shield. Edwin stopped the car with a screech of tires. His arm
shot protectively across Simon's chest, though Simon's head still
tapped the dashboard lightly. When Simon looked up, the truck
driver had climbed out of the cab and was examining something beneath his vehicle.

"Wait here, don't come out," Edwin said to Simon as he
joined the other driver at the side of the road, where they
examined the ground, looking grave and shaking heads. Simon
peeked over the hood of the Reliant, on which the fedora now
lay, and could see what he thought were rose petals and white
driftwood crushed together in a red and white paste, from
which sprouted a callused, black foot. It took him a few seconds
to realise that the driftwood and haemorrhaging roses were the
mangled leg of the man who had materialised at the side of the
road. When his father returned, they reversed, pulled out in
front of the truck, and sped along the road to a nearby farm
from where Edwin telephoned for the police and ambulance—
the ambulance being a mere formality and transport to the
morgue.

Later, Simon heard rumours about the man's death: that he
had thrown himself in front of the truck because his land had
been appropriated by the government. He had no children, no
wife, and people said that as a child he had been ill and so his
sex didn't function and he wanted to end the rest of his
functions as well. Other people said that they'd seen him having
sex with the goats he'd kept. Some avoided the subject of the
man himself, but joked that on the east coast road it was better

to hit a man than a pig—pigs, when they burst, excreted a treacherous oil that could cause tires to spin out of control and cause severe accidents and possibly death.

"That's bunk," Simon's father said. "Don't listen to that kind of bunk." Simon knows now, from the cold tingle in his toes, which have lost their sandpaper glow, how much his father had wanted to deny what had been going on in Guyana at the time, how much he had wanted to stay. He knows that the first story was the truth, that the man had lost everything, had nothing to live for if he didn't have his land, and that deterioration was hobbling toward their country like the twisted leg of slavery.

Simon dips his hand into his pocket to touch the compass he has been carrying, and he remembers his father's distracted state during this period, and his own vague foreboding about events swirling around them. He had watched his father's face tighten at news reports on the radio, at stories of violence and the misfortunes of people in the countryside, and Simon sensed the chaos that was undermining the spirit of some and igniting that of others.

The broom and the cup. They were the symbols of the two rival parties, the PNC and PPP, racially delineated black and Indian, the first one promising to sweep out all the decadence—tidy up a black state—the second one promising to feed the poor—Indian broth. The broom and the cup were the symbols that would appear on the ballots at the voting booth—simple, decipherable messages for the illiterate. When the broom ruled, the supporters of the cup suffered, and vice versa. One of Edwin's clients, an East Indian man in Rose Hall who kept horses and grew rice, had been producing Grade #1 rice for twenty years before the party of the broom gained power and graded his crop a #3. On the day he received notice of his new standing, he took a bottle of rum to his home above the confectionery store and threw his leather-bound ledger out the window,

scattering its unhappy figures in the middle of the road. He
stayed drunk for two days and never cultivated another grain of
rice. When Simon and his father visited him, the man was
nostalgic about the days of Empire, before independence.
"Them was different days—good days, doc," he said to Edwin
while holding his own hands together in a prayer. "What
missin' is prayer dees days, doc. Hindu and Muslim and
Christian should still pray, all on de same day—don' matter
which is de day, just pray."

Simon knows that his father filed away these events so that
when the extremist polemics of Guyana politics lashed out near
his own family, the incidents spilled out in fast forward,
propelling him into a future outside of his country, a country
whose waterfalls were his tears, whose savannahs were his
breath.

Simon remembers the day perfectly. It was a Saturday in
Stabroek market, the smell of fresh-baked patties wafting from
stalls and people pushing through the aisles choosing fresh
produce that came in weekly from the country. "*Where de
lizard, teacher lizard . . .*" Calypso blared from one of the stalls
selling records. After their shopping and a small battle of wills
in which Edwin told David he could not buy a record—"*you
know the lizard musse ticklin' she*"—the family headed home. At
the exit from the market, a group of PNC party members
wielding brooms made of thick straw stopped traffic with a
rally demonstrating their confidence in winning the coming
election. The Carters, stuck in traffic, waited for the parade to
pass. Curious, the children decided to get out of the car to have
a better look. Edwin encouraged them, against their mother's
wishes. "Don' fret, Grace," said Edwin. "It's good education for
them," and joined his children at the corner. Grace stayed alone
in the car, presentiment curling in her brow.

The demonstration was a spectacle of drums and horns, like
a carnival, but instead of feathers and fans, the participants

waved placards and flags and brandished brooms, sweeping the air in a gesture of what was to come. One man jumped on the roof of a car and used his broom to bar others from joining him, pushing them back onto the road. It reminded Simon of a game he had played on a mound of dirt in their yard in Kitty: "*I'm the King of the castle, and you're the dirty rascal.*"

A sudden whisk of air, the sharp smell of straw, and then a broom swept before his eyes, brushing his forehead. In the same second came a deep whimper from beside him. Simon turned to see David's cheek split open like a ripe peach. There was commotion and pushing. Someone pulled Simon out of the way. Francie shrieked and ran back to the car pulling Maggie by the hand. Simon saw his father bend down to pick up the sharp straw that had flown from the broom. Edwin examined it and touched the blood on its tip, wiping it from his fingers into his trousers, and then he hustled the boys back to the car and to the hospital. The doctors there assured them that the cut to David's face was not as bad as it might have been, but stitching was necessary and there would likely be scarring.

Simon sat patiently with his sisters on the wooden bench in the corridor; Grace stood by the door waiting for the doctors to finish. A tall woman like her English grandfather, she seemed, to Simon, to tower over everyone else in the hospital. Balancing on her left leg she would rub her right foot to the back of her calf, pushing up the hem of her skirt. It was a twitch she repeated every two or three minutes throughout the duration of the wait. Her calf became red and chafe at the spot her shoe rubbed it up and down. Her face didn't betray anxiety when she turned to glance at her children; she even managed a smile and a wink. Finally, David emerged with his face bandaged. The children piled silently into the Reliant; at home, Grace treated them to ice cream and tamarind candies.

After that day, a granular, dusty despondence grew in Edwin. He had believed in progress, but also in order. When the broom party won the election, Edwin and Grace would talk late into the night, and Grace's letters and calls to relatives increased. A few months later the Carters were on a boat to Barbados, an island that Simon had heard was more British than England—a slow, orderly place with no waterfalls and no riots. In the cabin of the steamer, Simon's father wept as they left the coast, as though pouring himself along with the Demerara and the Essequibo into the ocean.

In Barbados, David blossomed into adolescence, and his new scar, which crossed the tip of his eye and pulled it farther in a slant, was like a mark of a seasoned street fighter, which he used to his advantage with girls and with new friends who would listen, mesmerised, to the embellished tale of the scar's origin. He grandstanded it and learned to walk with a strut that escorted the mark handsomely.

The China scar on his brother's cheek reminded Simon of the ritual symmetrical cuts on the faces of African men he has seen in the subway. Dark and round against the coffin-white satin, David's face was an incomplete mask, the echo of a lonely darkness. A sacrificial face. Simon touched David's skin and a cold rubbery irony tingled up the tip of his finger.

From the couch at the back of the funeral parlour, Simon watched his mother as she stood in front of David's coffin. Without Edwin beside her she appeared shorter. Her face creased in a scowl. When she bent to say something to David's body, Simon watched her legs and counted, *one, two, three,* as she raised her right toe to scratch her left calf.

CHAPTER 2

Water

Faye has been practising a fugue. It's comforting in the wake of death, because it has answers—the subject posed, completed, answered, then repeated. Point and counterpoint. No mystery. David's death is symphonic, catastrophic, and resonant of nineteenth-century orchestrations. She wonders if he would appreciate the dialogue of this fugue, this *Kunst der Fuge* by Bach. David was walking music, free-jazz, heady and groiny. It oozed out, attracting some people to him and repulsing others. Arms like snakes hissing through the air—*sssss strike, sssss strike.* She rosins her bow.

Faye first saw David on stage in a bar in Toronto's west end; his arms were slithering over bongo drums. Her friends had cajoled her into coming with them to see Scorpio play during Caribana. "This is exactly what's been missing from your life," said Christine, who had met the saxophone player in Barbados and was eager to show him off. It was an obvious attempt to distract her. Faye had been trying to banish the shadow of Michael after having recently left him, but the resistance had hollowed out a space where music had once been. Her other friend, Mary, rightly feared that Faye might fall back under the spell of all those old notes and the hormone-popping experiments she had put herself through trying to get pregnant. Mary had been insistent and had waited while Faye reluctantly brushed on brown eyeshadow before they left to meet Christine and Emma.

The performance was part of a Caribbean festival always staged during the insistent humidity of August. The bar was packed and the air conditioning couldn't keep up with the press of bodies. *Sssss strike, sssss strike.* Steel drums gonged in the hollow chamber of Faye's breast. Mary and Christine swayed their hips as they listened to the rhythmic fusion of reggae and Motown that was the trademark of Scorpio. Emma bounced beside Faye, who focused on the music, holding on to her musical training. She tried to hear the music the way a conductor would and analyse its cadences and rhythmic singularity. *Tap, tap* . . . Michael's white baton on the black music stand. Wait, wait . . . his arm, wait for his arm . . . down . . . now play. She counted, beating off a conductor's vantage point on Scorpio. The music was simplistic, merely about the body. Nothing in the caressing of animal hide was complicated enough to elevate it to art—inspiration and improvisation were mutually exclusive. There, done. *Tap, tap* . . . arms fall, enough. She had named it and put it in its place. She swigged her beer, placed it back on the bar, and tugged at the label on the bottle, feeling smug.

During the intermission the band members slinked up and spread around Faye and her friends at the bar. Her girlfriends flirted, their imagination blowing a tropical breeze through their hair; now and then they'd flip it away from their eyes. *So exotic.* James, the sax player, bought drinks. The bongo player, introduced to them as David, piped up from his spot along the bar:

"Now which one of ya'll is the whore and which one the angel? I want to get 'dat one straight so I don' end up with the angel, because, laud, dem angels does wreck one havoc 'pun me balls. All that heavin' and fuckin' at holy air, man it hurt bad."

Silence. Measuring his effect. Ready. Then his face slowly folded back in an ear-to-ear grin, teeth splayed, the scar across his eye adding another laugh line to his rippled cheeks. Faye fidgeted on her stool and concentrated on the label of her bottle. Her friends stared mortified into their umbrella-trimmed glasses. David seemed to wait for an answer, his prominent mouth moving gradually from a grin to a naughty tongue-in-cheek. Smoke rings hung about the women's heads.

The silver label with the caribou head came away from Faye's beer bottle. Virgin. According to the adolescent folklore, if you could tear the label off a beer bottle in one piece, you were a virgin. If not, well, clearly you were not. Faye had never been sure if it was a good or a bad thing to be seen peeling off a fully intact label, but she had managed to do it every time she tried.

"Allow me to apologise for my brazen friend, ladies. He is no gentleman," said James finally, holding tight onto his accent and squeezing the word gentleman out through his teeth.

"Fa' sure. We say he wasn't brought up right by he motha, but then we meet some a' he family and they's sweet as sugar, so we don' know what wrong wid he," said the drummer, shaking his head, sending his braids swinging.

Faye's friends accepted the lame apologies, not wanting to give any more thought to the man's rudeness. But the oppositions challenged Faye, caging her the same way the doctor's utterance of the word "infertile" had defined her, and roused her to confront him.

"And what if we're both? Or neither?"

"Now that would be a first darlin', and I would praise both god and the devil right here . . ." he pointed to the floor.

"Assuming they had anything to do with it in the first place," she shot back.

"You tellin' me otherwise?" David stared at Faye earnestly, as though waiting to hear a secret from which he'd been barred until that very moment. His voluptuous lips, ribbed like a perfect seashell, parted slightly. A vulnerability escaped from beneath his bravado, and for a moment Faye felt an urge to shelter what she understood in him.

Whores and angels. David's binary opposition reminded Faye of a boy she had once met in a bar. Faye is very tall, taller than most women at a gangly five foot ten. At fourteen she could pass for eighteen or older and could dress her way into bars, restricted movies, coffee houses to hear folk singers among left-over hippies, and before the gazes of older men. Music was everywhere. Faye remembers feeling that being a woman meant being a cactus tree, full and hollow, like the lyrics Joni Mitchell sang. She met Rick at the Colonial Tavern, where she and two girlfriends had blown their allowances on the ten-dollar cover charge to see a band. He invited her to dance. Slow dancing. With boys her own age, she had made sure their shoulders never touched and had kept her groin far out of reach. But Rick pulled her close and she gave in to his body. His hands slid down her waist and held her buttocks. They ground to a love song.

"I like my women skinny," he said into her ear. No response from Faye, just the furl, furl, furl, of mascaraed eyelashes. "There are two types of women, there are skinny ones, and then there are mothers. Mothers are always ripplin' out of their shirts and their shorts as if they're storing up flesh in order to multiply and have more of 'emselves walking on the street."

Faye remembers this with a slight ache. She pinches her waist . . . *this? this? this spindly flesh under splotchy skin . . . is this what has sentenced me? Push, push.*

Through the entire dance she took quick, shallow breaths, afraid that her chest would heave full and maternal. Everything still except her eyelashes, *furl, furl.* He introduced himself, said that he worked as a plumber and made lots of money, and then went on to describe in detail the cottage he was building on Balsam Lake. Not daring to look anywhere else, especially not up at her girlfriends, she stared at his neck, the skin dry and fallow but for a mole protruding from behind his ear. She became unnaturally thirsty. The song was never going to end. When it finally did there was another, even slower . . . *short, short breaths.*

She returned to the table after the second dance, and before her friends had a chance to quiz her, she gulped down her Singapore Sling, grabbed her purse and said come on, let's go. The others bundled up sweaters and purses and followed her,

running out of the bar, their fourteen-year-old selves rematerial-
ising in that moment of escape from unnamed adult obscenities.
Out in the street, Faye described the encounter, from the touch
of Rick's large hands on her bony bottom to the waves of
cigarette and beer breath. She could tell them of the feel of his
chest against hers and the tremor the words spoken in her ear
had sent through her, but she couldn't describe for those eager
ears the sight of the mole sprouting three, wiry black hairs on
the desert of his skin.

It was this feeling of confused confidence that David had
stirred in her. In the wide-eyed tone of David's voice she sensed
a crack, a blemish not unlike the mole: not something she could
see, but something that came up invisibly through him,
chinking his lusty armour. As a sound he would have been the
din of a cracked cymbal. *Waaoong.*

In the second set David sang. His voice was clear and
strong, his phrasing as natural as breathing. The bar hushed. The
song was angry and erotic, unsettling. Halos of smoke hung
high above the stage. David's dark eyes were shut, but Faye
noticed around them a trace of hopeful feminine adolescence,
simultaneously angry and vulnerable. She started to perspire.
She tugged at the label of a new beer bottle but stopped short
of peeling it off as she glanced back at David's exposed shoulders
and the peanut-shell curves of his arms.

How different he was from Michael. Within a few minutes
David had exposed more to her—a stranger—than had Michael
in all their years together. In Michael Faye had searched for
cracks that would echo her own vulnerability; she was eventually forced to invent them. Michael could conduct himself
the way he did the orchestra, all controlled emotion, spreading
himself over the instruments like a blanket of skin.

Ta . . . ta . . . ta dum . . . harpsichord and strings in unison—
urgent. Undeniably Mozart. The flute in the second bar enters

like condolence, breaking the tension. The pain of change shoots to Faye's chest. The Bartok is finished and one of her oldest CDs has slid into play. She picks up her cello bow and moves to the full-length mirror in her room. She raises both arms, and slices the air of memory, closing her eyes, conducting Mozart's aria.

"*Misero . . . o sogno . . .*"

[. . . harpsichord . . . more violently now, and horns . . . now, second violin, come in . . . slowly . . . a wave . . .]

"*Oh, my unhappiness . . . the home of shadows . . .*

"*Open this infernal door . . . open it merciless beings . . . no one can hear me, and alone . . .*"

The lament dwindles; the pace picks up. Her bow slices wider, faster, bringing all the instruments together . . . then a rest, now strings in double time. Faye can feel the strain in her arm as she guides all the notes herself.

They had been so young.

Michael had been the youngest professor in the music department. When he stood at the front of the room, the class fell silent. They waited. The moment he started talking was like the first beat. He lowered his hands to grasp the sides of the lectern and they were all in his control, listening and writing at his command. They say a conductor is born, not made, and each movement of Michael's body proved that true. He was dark will, all energy. An olive face, massive brow, thick eyebrows over deep eyes, an affirming nose and keen mouth. Don Giovanni, Faye thinks now. A character inconceivable in words, but manifest in music, in his insistent D-minor "*No! No! No! No!*" the final refusal before his downfall. Like the mysterious power of Don Giovanni over Donna Anna in Mozart's opera, Michael was the music that seduced Faye. She surrendered to the notes. For someone who had learned all her opera from Bugs Bunny, Michael appeared as a scribe, coding and decoding her early experiences, putting words like "motif" and "recitatif" to child-hood images of Bugs in black tie and tails conducting the anvils dropping on Elmer Fudd. *Figaro, Figaro, Fiiigaaarooo. Smack.*

Faye took all the courses Michael taught, trying to soak him in. She asked questions that would impress him, but he remained distant. He never looked at her and in doing so made her love him. It was two years after she graduated with her B.A.—after she had returned from the futile Paris trip—that they met at a music department party. Surrounded as he was by young women, Michael took no notice of Faye for most of the evening, until she summoned the courage to offer him a drink.

"I see you're drinking Scotch. Like another?"

"Well, indeed I would. Thank you."

As she handed back the glass the ice was jiggling to the tempo of her trembles. Faye waited for a moment of recognition . . . *one beat, then two, three, four* . . . the bar ran out of notes.

"After your course, I went to Paris."

"My course?"

Pause, one, two . . .

"Oh yes, you . . ."

He claimed to remember her, and told her later that he had often thought about her, but she now suspects he hadn't at all. When she went home with him that night to his duplex near the university, it seemed natural, a progression as though it had been written for them, and Faye, like Donna Anna in her exalted state of agitation, succumbed. She stayed for almost a decade, not to deny or avenge as Donna Anna had Don Giovanni, but to become an extra pair of ears that would listen to the music Michael conducted and loyally affirm it.

Faye rests the bow on the music stand.

Nannerl skips in again. While travelling throughout Europe in the road-show of their early lives, Nannerl Mozart and her brother were often ill one after the other. In 1765 Nannerl fell ill with typhus of the stomach, recovering two months later. That month, Mozart was similarly afflicted and didn't fully recover until the spring of 1766. Two years later they both contracted smallpox, both recovering, although Nannerl's recovery was somewhat speedier than Wolfgang's. In all the biographies of Mozart, Nannerl is described as his "pale sister" whose journal entries, in contrast to the humorous, parodic, scatological writings of her brother, are said to be dry and unemotional. "If one cannot say a thing," says Wittgenstein, "one must be silent about it." Were Nannerl's noises in some unwritten music? By the day Nannerl was married to her baron, Mozart had already composed numerous symphonies, sonatas, divertimenti, and was beginning *The Marriage of Figaro*. Nannerl lived to a ripe old age.

Only when Faye started to play music again did she recognise that the years with Michael were a great silence, despite her technical progress in the orchestra, where she sat at the last desk in the cello section thanks to Michael's nepotism. The years of too many notes. Like David she had been off-balance, simultaneously seasoned and naive. David's confusions and contradictions resembled her own, but with a different accent. She disliked him for it, but there in the bar his magnetism was sucking up the metal filings of her silence.

After David's band finished playing, her friends were reluctant to leave. Mary was now thoroughly drunk and rested her head on the bar that was being cleared of its bottles and glasses. Christine and Emma idled their way to the stage to talk to James and the rest of the band. They paused on the brink of curiosity, but the *thud, thud* of drums still in their chests led them all to David's apartment.

More drums and rhythms, but these were erotic, with the same muted intensity of the candlelight. Faye felt she'd made a mistake in coming, thinking there'd be a bigger party than just

the four women and two of the band members. She watched
David as he lit candles and moved the furniture aside to create
a dance floor. They avoided eye-contact, which they'd been
doing since their exchange in the bar. When he pulled her up
to dance, he looked her straight in the eyes, hopeful. Her face
burned, but she diverted her gaze to the wall behind him. Her
reluctant feet shuffled along beside his capable step. He swayed
her. She was dizzy, but her body had never felt so attached to
the downbeat, and she was slipping toward this new music. She
sought out the comfort of her musical training, but when she
pictured Michael's arms the baton was off the beat. The image
of the hoary mole on Rick's neck popped up—the dry territory
of her innocence—and she pulled back abruptly from David.

Surprised, he stood still, then threw up both his arms, his
palms raised and his head cocked, indicating "no pressure." But
he looked frightened. Faye feared she'd been rude and was
about to make an excuse, but he disappeared into the kitchen,
returning with a beer in hand. He looked over at Emma, who
was obviously wanting to dance. He hesitated, but when she
gave him a wide smile he held out his hand. Emma leapt up and
into his embrace, eagerly pressing her groin to his. They danced,
barely moving, their hips tight and their pelvises grinding:
right, then left, right, left, right . . . the *chisel, chisel* of rubbing
bones. It didn't take them long to disappear into the bedroom.
James and Christine continued to dance near the open window
that led from the living room out to a fire escape.

Finding it hard to breathe, Faye retreated to the kitchen
where Mary sat at the table, throwing coins from the table to
the floor. They started a guessing game. Mary would toss coins
against the wall and as they bounced to the tile floor, Faye, eyes
closed, would guess their denomination from the sound
echoing through the empty kitchen.

"Quarter."

"No, that was a nickel. Drink."

"OK, nickel. Next?"

"Try this one."

With each correct guess, Mary had to take a drink; Faye would drink if she guessed wrong. Thanks to her exceptional hearing Faye was staying superbly sober, while Mary, who had revived on the way to the apartment, was slurring more words with each swig of beer.

"A dollar, for sure, that had a heavy copper sound . . . Loony."

"Right, my drink."

"Go ahead, I'm headed for a wining streak. Next toss."

"You'll never get this one."

"A dime, a thin dime, you can hear it's a higher pitch, like a high chime in a clock, definitely a dime."

"Right again, not bad, my drink."

Clink, clink, then a door flew open . . . *bang,* against a wall. A shuffling body made its way down the hall. A man appeared, wearing only his shorts, squinting in the glare of the fluorescent light.

"That's my wall you're knocking on," he said, his voice clouded with the phlegm of sleep.

"Oh shit, sorry," said Mary, giggling, then slapping her hand over her mouth.

He stood blinking them into focus, trying to recognise the two women and wondering what to do next.

Inhale. "We're really sorry," Faye said. "We had no idea. We're leaving anyway—let's go Mare."

"Please, not on my account," he threw in before they could get up. "I'm up now anyway. I won't get back to sleep before the sun comes up. That's just the way it is."

Faye noted something different about him. Exhale. "Oh, great, I feel better now, your whole night ruined rather than just part of it." She smiled, an offering of parted lips that might make him smile back.

He was slow to pick up her cue, but a beat later jumped in: "Sounds like you've done this before . . ."and then teeth, large square front teeth that said *OK, I'll play.* "I'm glad at least I'm dealin' with an expert who could do a thorough job."

"At your service," she added, pushing this just a little too far but feeling comfortable with this stranger.

"I'm used to these parties now. Or at least I should be. Sorry if I sounded gruff." He raised his right hand and gestured over his shoulder in a backward wave indicating the past, and Faye noticed the tiny bones of his hands, the delicate knuckles and long fingers. Unusual for a man. She realised what was different about him. It was a trace of old-world manners and breeding even at three in the morning. Breathe, breathe. He wasn't as tall as David, but had his build, the curve of muscular shoulders balancing rolling, hairless pectorals. His legs were firm, calves slightly bowed, athletic. His eyes resembled David's, curiously slanted just at the edges of his face, but he was fairer than David, coffee not chocolate, his hair not kinky, but tightly curled. He had a large flat nose and the most perfectly curved and voluptuous lips. She passed her tongue over her own.

"You've been here before, haven't you?" he asked her. She shook her head and looked down at the hands in her lap, and then, quickly, back up at his. He caught her staring and folded his arms across his bare chest, suddenly uncomfortable.

"Excuse me," he said, politely, and walked out of the room with an uneven gait. Faye and Mary exchanged a guilty look.

He returned buttoning a white cotton shirt and introduced himself as Simon, David's younger brother.

"You live here too?" Mary asked through a wide yawn. Faye's eyes followed Simon's fingers up the button line of his shirt.

"Just for now. I was working in Alberta, and I had a very stupid accident." He looked down at his foot. "Stepped in an animal trap, broke it."

The limp. He told them that several months before, after
the accident, he had returned to Barbados to see if he could
remake his life there. Now he was working in a meat-packing
plant in the west end. He rambled through these details as if
reporting for duty. Faye's eyes flicked between his hands and the
broken foot, while his eyes shyly darted about the room. When
they shot her way, Faye inspected his long, curved lashes
enviously. Her first pang for David was being drowned by
Simon's depth.

"David has a lot of friends," he said timidly as he pulled out
a chair to sit down.

"And you?"

"No, not really. I don't make them that fast." His voice was
soft and lilting, not brash like his brother's, his accent
consciously curbed.

Faye waited for a resonance. Simon was a solid bronze bell.
She knew that when he was rung the air would surge and
vibrate down to bedrock, a deep tolling she wanted to hear. Her
lungs were expanding.

"Why didn't you stay in Barbados?"

His eyebrows came closer together as he considered his
answer. Oops, had her question cut too close?

"I mean, I don't really know much about Barbados, except
that it's popular with tourists," she continued guiltily, knowing
the island's reputation with some Canadian women who went
there to get "big bamboo." Breathe. Breathe.

"There's a story back home about a lizard, a story from over
twenty years ago . . ." Faye noticed his accent become more
pronounced.

"We've a lot of very expensive hotels on the west coast,
with restaurants where things are very proper, jacket and tie, a
little snooty . . . back then especially. One night during the
evenin' meal two English women were dinin' on flying fish,

their silver cutlery scrapin' the bone china. People were warmin' up with rum punch—tourists aren't used to it, comes on suddenly—and the talk got louder, people loosened up. The two ladies were almost finished their fish. As the last mouthful was raised to one woman's lips, all of a sudden a cockroach ran across the table and disappeared under the tablecloth. Both ladies shrieked, I mean loud, loud, and dropped their forks at the same time. One of the women called over the waiter and complained. They made a big fuss saying they're never comin' back, shite like that. The whole restaurant was watching them now. More hotel staff came around. Managers, and people just findin' out what the fuss was about. They calmed the ladies down, and just as things were about to get back to normal, the roach reappeared at the centre of the table. It was large, people say: two joints on a forefinger long. Then, in the next second, something else appeared on the table. A lizard. In a sudden swoop, the lizard pounced on the roach and crunched it in its mouth, chewin' and swallowing while everyone around the table and even the other guests watched, completely in shock. Perfect silence then. And all of a sudden, a swelling sound . . . *whoop! whoop!* The waiters burst into whoops like they would have if a run had been scored by the West Indies. They applauded the lizard like he was a star batter and their cheers carried throughout the restaurant and echoed in the pans of the steel drums on the stage."

He stopped. Faye watched him and waited, but he had finished. She had no idea what bearing the story had on her question, but she wanted more: *Describe the hiss of cicadas; tell me the smell of your mother's fever-checking hand on your forehead; tell me the name you gave your fear of the dark.* Months later when talking about his childhood, he told her that the lizards which used to climb the inside walls of his house were disappearing. Only then did she make a possible connection.

But that night her nervousness jumped into his silence, and

she told him about her telemarketing work: everything from corporate clients to theatre subscriptions—showtime in those first moments on the telephone: "Mrs. Rosedale, is culture something missing from your life?" A while later she heard a door open down the hall and the *slap, slap* of large bare feet on the wooden floor. David walked into the kitchen, the elastic waistband of his boxers folded under, pulled up in sleepy haste. He squinted into the light.

"Eh, eh, Simon . . . you up?"

"Well, forced up, by me," said Faye, looking at one then the other, nervously.

"Tek care boy," David said as he opened the fridge and took out a carton of orange juice, "that one's one they ain' told us about yet . . . or so she says . . . *he, he.*" He tilted his head back to gulp down the juice.

Simon looked at Faye, but she stared at him blankly. He looked back down at the floor. David returned the empty carton to the fridge, closed the door, and turned around. He glanced at Mary who had nodded off in her chair, chin in her chest and a trickle of drool slipping down from her lips.

"It's horrible when sleep's humiliating," Faye said in Simon's direction, joking. *Please smile, please laugh . . . I want to hear.* David chuckled and then shuffled back down the hall to the bedroom and closed the door. Faye looked at Simon. The mood had changed in the room.

"What would you have done in Barbados?"

"Not sure. Things go on without you," he said heavily in the way she has now come to recognize, a shift that narrows and deepens him like a cleft in rock, the one she would eventually come to know how to fill, the aphrodisiac of his fatigue that would always suck her down into him. But then it was new and she skipped across the mood. When he asked her more about herself, she began to talk about music. Their conversation was carried out at a remove. In the foreground were Simon's thin, elegant hands, his right thumb scraping the table, his left hand coming up to touch his face, rub his neck. Faye's left hand was holding the still full, warm beer bottle; her right hand tore at its label, trying to remove it in one pull but, for once, whorishly ripping it off in pieces, shredding the caribou's head. Their hands played, a kind of dance without touching skin to skin. Four-handed music. The sun was coming up.

She pushes the rest of the memory back. She feels an ache growing in her throat—the pain of the first moments of love. Pain nonetheless. She examines her right palm, rubbing new creases—harrowed, episodic lines. She thinks that in the past seven years it's been their hands that have kept them together, silently groping for the other's in the dark, in a crowd, at the cinema. Simon has taken her hand from the thermometer, shaken the instrument down to zero, and led her to bed to defy the odds and make a child. Hope and trust. But since Paris, their hands have remained mostly by their own sides, fearful, dangling at the end of arms like vestigial talons.

David is buried. His band, Scorpio, disbanded long ago. Faye wonders who is resting tonight. Which people at the funeral are sleeping already? Is suicide ever hermetic? Are the members of the rotary club revisiting their prank? The police chief, she imagines, is still awake. Simon hasn't slept for the last three nights. "That's just the way it is," as he said that first night. When he doesn't sleep, he and Faye are even further apart. Wide, wide noises. In the last two years, they have made love twice, and only very recently, when she thought the timing was right to conceive. She gets up from the floor and goes to the door. I should see if he's all right, down in the cold basement. *Maybe tonight? Maybe tonight.*

The smell of her hair is bonded to Simon's nostrils. The mint tea and honey she brought is steaming on the desk beside his arm. He is alone again, embarrassed by her attempts to comfort him. Faye had rested her hands on his shoulders and offered to give him a massage but, "Later," he said and thanked her with a feeble smile. Her smell tempted him. He hurries his hand up under his shirt to feel his chest for the heart beat, wanting to feel it skip the way it used to when she was near him. He rubs his cold fingers over the warm skin and waits for the irregular pulse that first told him that she had stolen a beat of his life, replaced every two seconds of life with the thought of her, the smell of her, the flutter of her laugh. He had begun to live inside her. What he feels is a steady pulse and a loitering guilt for not trying harder, for suspecting Faye of ulterior motives, of wanting his sperm and not his soul, but this has been the tenor of their brushes with each other lately. The spontaneity of lust is suppressed.

Lust and children and families—so deceptively simple and natural, the way it was for Simon's father, the way family fell into place for Edwin like the perfect *V* of a flock aligning itself along the horizon. But the perfection of the *V*-formation is marred now that Edwin is alive to witness the death of his first born.

Simon has seen the future. Fluorescent and fast, healthy and sterile—the future into which his children would be born. Was that why he hesitated with Faye that night? A month ago Faye asked him to join her on a night out—a gentle gesture to help them move forward as a couple, and he had agreed with an enthusiasm that surprised him. And even when they arrived at the new, four-story complex, he felt a rush of optimism. One-stop entertainment. Everything a family would desire under one roof. On the first floor was a General Motors showroom, with computer displays of virtual cars of the future that could be zoomed down yet-to-be-built highways. On the second floor was Fanamoto—a fast-paced Japanese-Californian restaurant—where they punched their order into a computer at the table, then were promptly delivered fried noodles with prawns and tofu. On the third floor, in a salon of two hundred grand fauteuils attached to individual video screens, they watched movies separately, Faye choosing a documentary about the Cuban Missile Crisis, and Simon a love story. After the film they ran their hands along fluorescent-coloured sedans and vans. Colours became tangible, as though artificial light had congealed on hoods and doors. Simon took it all in, trying to design a legend to the map that was taking shape in his brain, but the compass points eluded him, and he went home with a head full of distorted colours, smells, and sounds.

When they got home, Faye hurried to the bathroom and after a few minutes she called to him from the top of the stairs. It was good timing, she said. They should make love.

Panicked, he undressed in the living room, throwing his clothes on the couch; then he crept up the stairs, faltering at the sight of her waiting under the covers, a ray of fear circling her face. Her long leg wrapping around him as he joined her caused a shiver. When he turned to kiss her, her eyes were closed. She lay before him like a child preparing to blow out the candles on a cake, wishing from the depths of her being—a child wishing for a child. Despite her caresses he remained limp, unmoved by her kind, hopeful mouth on his and along his thighs. He tried to concentrate but could see only the building with the four storeys, the spray of light from the cars. He tried to think of something else, something warm and erotic, and finally he settled on the sea at home, at Consett Bay . . . and the casuarina trees. The lick of surf on a granular beach, the random deposits of wood and lace-like rock . . . It was working. He began to feel a tingling in his pelvis. The salt breath wind . . . He took her breast in his hand and raised it to his mouth. The sun was reflecting off the cliff. A salt breeze wafted from her skin. The sound of a seabird . . . a pelican, no, dozens of them, circling, happy and hungry. Diving. No. Fear struck him then. The pelicans. They had come in large numbers that first sighting; after that there had been fewer, and later even fewer. *Where had they . . . ?* No. He pushed her aside. "I'm sorry," he said. "I'm just very tired." She stared at him, disbelieving. Her face crumpled and she turned away from him. The pelicans flew above the cliffs, scanning the sea for fish. Even as he watched Faye's shoulders heave with stifled sobs, Simon could not comfort her or try again. *Water dissolves an old form either to create a new form or annihilate it. Salt is an unknown and invisible body, like a spirit that sustains the thing which it permeates.* The pelicans dove for fish but some never broke the surface again. Could science explain what had happened? Faye's breathing gradually evened out, then grew heavy, and she soon began to snore.

Faye stares at herself in the long mirror. She sees roundness where there wasn't any before. Turning sideways, she pushes the air from her lungs into her belly to make it big and bloated, but she is too thin. Grabbing a cushion from the chair, she places it under her shirt. Sideways again. Pregnant.

She will be forty in a month. Barrenness creeps towards her like a dry lizard. Unlike Simon, she has not had the kind of family to swim through, to submerge in, and to resurface from the fluids of attachment. By the time her mother was forty she had already raised both Faye and her brother, and had appointed each independent. She then proceeded to have a nervous breakdown.

Wash the dishes, dry the dishes, turn the dishes over. Faye's father found her mother in the kitchen repeating this mantra, holding onto a dishtowel that she had tugged at and twisted until it was almost in shreds. Returning late in the evening from the racetrack, he had no idea how long she'd been in that state.

"*Wash the dishes, dry the dishes, turn the dishes over,*" she greeted her husband.

"Sandra?" Faye can hear the Irish dip in his voice.

"*Wash the dishes, dry the dishes, turn the dishes over,*" she answered.

"What's going on, love?" He approached her and grasped the dishtowel to take it from her.

"*WASH THE DISHES, DRY THE DISHES, TURN THE DISHES OVER!*" she hollered, holding tightly onto the rag.

Her father recoiled. He telephoned Faye and asked her to come home, saying only that her mother was behaving strangely. When Faye arrived at the small house in Etobicoke with the Derby horse on the mailbox, she walked slowly to the door, taking a *hop, hop* up the stairs as a way to defy what she sensed she was about to confront. Her mother greeted her with the dish rag. *Dry the dishes, dry the dishes.* By the time the decision to take her to the hospital was made, her mother's colour had turned bronze, her face statued in shock. Faye's father refused to go along, as though the shame was his and he sought to spare himself the humiliation. Faye was furious, but didn't dare raise her voice in front of her mother. They arrived at the hospital with Faye guiding her reluctant mother through the automatic doors. When anyone in emergency asked her mother a question, she repeated her ditty. Once, she smiled and shook her finger at an orderly with a scolding wag: "*turn the dishes oooooover.*"

After two months in the hospital, Faye's mother was sent home. She would speak and listen, but she rarely looked anyone in the eye. Faye moved back home during the first semester of her second year at university and did her best to keep an eye and ear out for any lapses in her mother, who spent most of her time replacing buttons, patching and darning old clothing. Faye's brother was living with his girlfriend and characteristically out of touch with the rest of the family. The stress soon took its toll on Faye's studies. She failed a score analysis course that she had to repeat the following summer, a setback she blamed on her mother for years to come. Her mother continued as an out-patient at the Clarke Institute for five years and, even after, blankness peeped out from under her heavy eyelids. Shifty eyes that the rest of her family could never trust. She began to shrink, her bones seeming to dissolve under wizening skin as she turned into an apple doll. When she died in her chair ten years ago, neither Faye nor her father and brother were surprised. It seemed natural that she would blow away one spring day like a seed from a tree.

Does the brain misfire from too little stimulation or from design? Is insanity the penalty of endowment, a levy on richness of spirit and mind? How could she account for the complexity of the sounds in her own head, the ones that later exploded into the burgeoning sounds of her own cells? *Not that . . . yet.* Had her mother's brain been so complex that the one-dimensionality that she finally achieved arrived like a blessing, a release from thought—everything reduced to the cleaning and turning of china? With an abortive wrench Faye pulls the pillow from under her shirt and flings it to the floor. Each of us our little madness we must handle.

She goes to the closet and pulls out a box. Cards, letters, bills, and photographs. Finally, this one. She sits on the floor, staring at the photograph of her family taken when she and her brother were not yet out of diapers, he just barely able to stand, with his father bending to hold his two tiny arms to balance him. They are in front of the falls at Niagara on a bright summer day. Her father looks strong, tanned, probably from long summer days at the racetrack. He looks like Edwin, Simon's father, the same watery eyes always on the verge of tearing up. Her father worked the early morning shift as a driver for the Toronto Transit Commission and at the end of each day would head to the racetrack. The track somehow reminded him of Ireland. As kids, it was all she and her brother ever knew of Ireland, that it was a place where horses sped around an oval turf trying to win money for their father. Her mother always joked with them that he loved horses more than he loved her, at least they thought it was a joke. Her mother, by contrast, is pale in the way a black and white photograph can make skin look undeveloped, verging on negative. A secret curls her lip up under her nose as though she is smelling it—not a real smile. Her eyes are opened wide, too wide for the brightness of the sky. Unnatural. Their feet seem to barely touch the pavement in front of the railing that separates them from the cascading tons of water. This photograph has a sound; it is an electric noise, a background hum of turbines like a fan threatening to clip the marionette strings that suspend them from the sky, so that they tumble on top of each other, limp and helpless.

Faye had always blamed her mother for the menacing hum. For a long time she represented something Faye had to endure, a nagging throbbing failure like a dying nerve in a tooth. Her fragility embarrassed Faye, who was determined to avoid her mother's fate and who could not bring herself to that delicate and patient friendship enjoyed by many women and their mothers. Her mother had seemed distant, selfish, and suspicious of her daughter, whereas with her son it appeared more as indifference. Faye hasn't seen her brother in almost ten years. He lives in New Orleans with his wife. They too are childless. *Clip, clip* . . .

By the time she was fifteen, Faye was sexually active. Always defiant of her mother's fragility, she strutted about the house in tight jeans and tops that exposed her tummy. One day after arriving home from school, her mother called her into the living room. It was a hot June day. School was almost over. Faye remembers the great anticipation, as though the day school was let out the future would become hers; she would be released into the sun like a sexy seal.

"Sit down," her mother said.

Faye slouched on the couch, chewing her gum loudly in hope of drowning out anything her mother might have to say.

"I used to have wings," she began. Faye rolled her eyes and stared at the wall.

"I'm serious. Not real wings, of course, but wings that attached to my boots at the ankles. My uncle made them for me—it was during the war, when I was seven. He told me he was going to India to play in Her Majesty's Royal Regiment Band and that if I ever wanted to see him, all I'd have to do was put on these wings and fly east. He'd eventually see me and send up a flare so I'd know where to land. He made the wings out of white silk that he ribbed with real quills from a white swan. He said, 'Swans could have been the best flyers if they hadn't let themselves get so fat, so don't you ever get fat or you'll never be able to fly.'

"I asked him to attach the wings to my favourite welling-tons. I went everywhere in them. The wings covered the sides of the boots and flapped when I ran. I flew and flew and flew—around the backyard, through the neighbourhood, over and above the city and the country. I was sure I could make it to India.

"One day while flying in the woods near our house, one of my wings caught on a twig and tore. I heard the noise as if it had been my own flesh that ripped and was left dangling on the twig. I limped homeward and on the way I met an older boy who lived a few houses away. He asked me why I was limping. 'I've broken a wing,' I explained. He laughed, but then stopped suddenly and said he knew how to fix wings. He'd fix it and it'd be good as new. My heart grew light. I would get to India after all. He took me into the shed at the back of his garden, where his father's tools were stored. He took down some glue and tape. He stood in front of me and said: 'If you want me to fix this wing, you'll have to do something for me in return. Nothing's free, you know.' I nodded. 'All I'm going to charge you is to have a look under your panties there. Pull them down and let me have a look.' I obeyed him. He looked. When he had seen whatever it is that he was looking for he turned his attention to my wing. He mended it with the glue. It flapped again when I put my boot back on. I didn't thank him. I flew home. The next day when I tried to fly in our yard I couldn't get off the ground. The wings didn't work. I ran and ran and ran but couldn't fly. How would I see the flare? I began to panic. *Send up the flare, send up the flare,* I cried. Maybe I'd find it if he sent up the flare now. Then I knew that I would never get to India. My uncle would think it was because I'd got fat. He told me not to get fat. How would I explain it to him? I broke the other wing and threw the whole lot in the trash."

Faye sat staring at her mother. *What the hell . . . ?* She had no idea. It seemed a pointless, silly story, and she was embarrassed at having listened to the whole thing. The first of her mother's secrets.

"Is that what you wanted to say?" Faye asked in her most surly tone.

"Yes, that's all."

Her mother looked away, out the living room window, feeling she'd done her highest duty. Faye got up from the couch abruptly. That night, she let the boy she was seeing push two fingers up inside her, and she took his penis in her hand and stared at it while he came.

These memories had been forgotten until just before her mother died, and then suddenly they revisited her along with flying dreams that were hormone-induced. At the time, she was with Michael and taking Perganol to make her ovulate. The drug had put her in a state between hell and euphoria, visiting one or the other without her control. In one dream, she was finally pregnant, and Michael was telling her what the doctor had just disclosed: "Five hundred dollars," he said, "they'll pay you five hundred for it, because there aren't enough abortions these days. The tissue can help with diabetes and Parkinson's." Scientists wanted to buy her fetus. She woke up crying for her mother. A few days later, her mother passed away.

Faye's father came to David's funeral as a courtesy to Simon who he seems to like a little more than Michael. He seemed almost merry, trying to help out with the crowd, ushering them into seats in the chapel. When he met Edwin he hugged him, and during the service he squeezed Faye's hand a number of times. She had the feeling he was trying to make up for her mother's funeral at which he'd remained mute, distant, wanting to sit at the back of the church, and even refusing afterward to drive with Faye and Michael to the cemetery.

In contrast to her mother's funeral, where Faye, her father, and her brother greeted a handful of mourners—some neighbours and a few visitors from Winnipeg, David's funeral was a public outpouring of grief. A crowd crammed into the chapel and spilled out onto the street. Simon's family, his relatives, their friends, all of whom were introduced to Faye as "auntie" or "uncle" despite the absence of a true blood tie, were present in full, plaintive sorrow. Many had travelled from the Caribbean; others now lived in Toronto. Great aunts and cousins, fathers and stepsons filed into the pews. Mothers wailed, running up to Simon's mother and throwing themselves around her, while their little girls in dark, elaborate dresses toddled after little child-men in suits and bow-ties that mocked their baby faces. The cause of this event was an affront to the foundation of their lives. "How could it happen? How could he have been so cut off, so alone, this wouldn't have happened back home, why didn't he confide in one of us, we're his family . . . *we're his family*."

Faye's father had ushered the police chief and his wife into one of the front pews. David's family watched them with suspicion. At first Faye was angry with her father's misplaced hospitality, but she remembered the warm words David had for the chief, how the man had welcomed him when he moved to Newmarket, how he had encouraged David to stay, to build a new life there. But the family had flanked along the left side of the chapel, barricading themselves with their shared mourning.

The desire that remains in Faye to build a family has none of the desperate obsession with self-completion it had in the days with Michael. It is more in line with the barricade she saw today in the faces of Simon's relatives, the sewing of a family garment that protects those inside from desperate angry hands that shred it in madness, in sadness, in misunderstanding. It is now a desire to plant the seed deeply, so that it can't blow away in the wind, a desire to reinstate the wings on a little girl so that when the flares go up she can land softly, intact, and at home in a foreign and exotic land.

CHAPTER 3

Salt

"Body fluids of meat and all a de elements that does make for putrefaction are drawn off by salting it, and so too all irrational desires of de body are banished by pious instruction." Simon was audience to MacKenzie's sermon; Maggie, naked in the sheet-metal tub set up in the carport for baths, was her captive congregation.

"A soul dat has not been salted with Christ's words will begin to smell and breed worms." MacKenzie wrung out the sponge. The soapy water ran down Maggie's forehead like a frothy benediction.

With her green eyes squeezed shut and her curls dampened, Maggie resembled the sea monkeys Simon used to see on packages that could be bought in the American store at the Hilton Hotel. The packages promised that with one wetting a sea monkey would sprout from the enclosed petri dish. But Simon had never seen an actual sea monkey; his father refused to give the children money to waste on such foolishness.

MacKenzie had wanted to bathe each of the children, but only Maggie could be bullied into the sudsy tub for the weekly scrub-down. She scrubbed Maggie's back and tiny arms until they were flaring pink. Maggie was starting to protest against this physical torture, as much because of her wish to be like her older siblings as the discomfort. She was growing up, testing her boundaries. Lately she had begun intercepting some of the folded Ting labels with lovesick illustrations that Best continued to float over shrubs to land at Francie's feet.

"Ow, that stings." Maggie pushed MacKenzie's fat arm from her shoulder and, wiping the soap from her eyes, sought to escape.

"Sit down, chile, we aren't finished. Simon come help with ya sista."

Simon reluctantly put down his bat. He had been practising in the sun, still determined to be the best batsman at Harrison College. They held the small squirming body in the tub each with one hand, and while MacKenzie scrubbed his sister's biscuit ringlets, Simon rinsed her down. As he dipped the rinse bucket in the tub, Simon spotted David sneaking out of the side door. In his arms was a drum—the drum that usually sat on a high shelf in the room they called the library, the African drum that had belonged to Simon's great, great grandfather and that the children were not allowed to touch. David picked his way over the asphalt, hoping to be invisible to the chaotic trio in the carport. Simon hurriedly upended the bucket over Maggie's head and tossed it into the tub, splashing water on MacKenzie's shift.

"Eh, eh, boy," she blurted, trying to keep a grip on the slippery Maggie. But Simon picked up his bat and was off, missing the rest of her tirade.

He followed David slowly at first, trying to decide whether or not he should catch up. Knowing that David should have been studying for his exams, Simon felt a wave of worry, even guilt, on his brother's behalf. With his right hand he reached down to where his buttocks met his thigh. It had been over a year since the day he broke the vase with the bat, but his father's lashes were buried deep in his backside. Edwin had given Simon two smart whacks with the horsewhip that lived at the back of the hall cupboard. The whip had been given to Edwin by a client in Berbice who raced horses that had never won a single race. "Needed a better rider, that's all. It did what it was told," said Edwin, defensively, to anyone who challenged his use of the instrument. Sometimes when Maggie knew she'd done something that would warrant the sting of the whip, she'd run to the closet before her father got home and bury the whip under the sheets and towels that shared the cherry wood shelves, hoping to delay the inevitable. All the children feared the whip and respected its authority. All of them, that is, except David, who was stretching out of adolescence and defied anything that stopped his desperate reach for adulthood.

David's passion for music excluded all else. He was preparing to write his A levels that spring, knowing that the exam results would determine his future. Over the course of months he ran a treadmill of quarrels with his father about his career, resisting the pressure to conform to Edwin's expectations. David had no interest in attending the University of Guelph in Canada to become a veterinarian like his father, nor would he compromise to study science, maths, or accounting at the University of the West Indies. He had his mind set. Music would set him free and he would reciprocate—composing, arranging, and recording a hybrid of Motown, rhythm and blues, reggae, and calypso. Only now does Simon understand the ingenuity of these ideas and how David was decades ahead of his time.

No one believed in David, least of all his father, who started to accidentally break records, accidentally walking over them if they were spread out on the floor, cracking them irreparably—accidentally—and denying the obvious. It was behaviour uncharacteristic of Edwin, something none of the family could credit him with doing intentionally, but suspicions grew when favourite albums disappeared, and, if asked, Edwin would merely shrug his shoulders.

Simon caught up to David along Garden Road. "Where you headed?" he asked shyly, always feeling green in his brother's presence.

"None of your business," David answered and kept walking.

David sped up, but Simon persisted despite David's backward glares and taunts to go back and play with Maggie. Finally, when they got to the main road, David stopped.

"Yuh not comin', Simon," he insisted and pointed back down the road to their house. Simon stood firm, trying to think of something to say. He thought of the time his father had discovered the missing condom, how silence had worked in his favour. Silence had reduced David's confidence to a sad puppy look of defeat. He tried it now, pushing back his shoulders slightly and holding his lips firmly together. A wave of confusion passed over David's face and Simon could tell it was working, that David was recognising Simon's tattletale power. Just a few more seconds and he would have victory. He pursed his lips a little tighter and moved his hand to his hip, summoning all his will to keep from trembling. David's shoulders dropped a fraction and he sighed, turned around and continued down the road.

Simon followed David as he headed up the main road toward St. Lawrence Gap. David walked quickly but Simon found it easy to keep up until David dashed between traffic to cross the road. The car fumes intensified the heat of the day. Simon's bare feet stung on the asphalt. A moke honked as he was about to cross the road. A mini-moke.

Simon feels a sharp stab of nostalgia.

Mini-mokes were new then, a tourist industry invention: Austin Minis without doors and with convertible tops—a tiny jeep for narrow back roads. The moke loaded with English tourists holding tight to the roll bar approached at a careful speed. As the vehicle slowed, one of the tourists pointed left for the others to take note of the donkey cart led by a vendor who sang "*Ackees for sale, ackees for sale . . . no yuh.*" Simon wanted to shout to the tourists that the fruits were really called guenips, but he didn't have the courage to speak up.

He smiles and sighs. He can't remember the last time he saw a donkey cart, or a bushel of ackees for that matter, and he knows they have gone the way of the coral reefs. Some of the fixtures of his childhood have completely disappeared from memory. When you juxtapose cartograms from different times for identical coordinates it is possible to see changes in the relative space. The thought of Barbados over the last twenty-five years exhausts him.

After the driver of the moke waved him across the road and sped off, Simon hopped his way along the hot cement of the narrow sidewalk. He heard the drum. David rapped the skin as he walked, and Simon followed the sound along the main road, past the Roti Hut and Sandy Beach apartments, past the Worthing police station and finally into St. Lawrence Gap toward the Church of St. Laurence. David veered left up the road along the sea, pounding the drum now, passing the new Royal Bank of Canada and the guest houses, passing Susie Yong's Chinese food restaurant, finally turning up the drive of a house on a small hill. Nat's house. The drumming stopped. David entered the house and Simon, not knowing what to do, waited on the road. He waited for almost half an hour, swinging his bat to pass the time. When David and Nat finally emerged they were carrying electronic equipment and musical instruments. They loaded up the car, got in, and backed it out into the road. The car stopped and the back door swung open. Simon leapt in and Nat sped off towards the east coast.

The south coast road edged the beaches, twisting past Oistins, then up beyond the airport, into St. Phillip, toward Sam Lord's Castle, a swing left to Oughterson and then right up toward the lighthouse at Ragged Point. They parked on the ridge.

"Ya might as well be of some help," said Nat, handing Simon a guitar and a small amplifier. Leaving his bat in the car, Simon followed the boys along a small dirt path down the cliff toward the sea. By the time they neared the bottom, David and Nat were sweating and panting.

A beach appeared, one Simon had never seen or knew existed. The path continued down to where the rock met the sand of a small cove, and there, hiding in the shrubs, stood a small chattel house whose rotted wood walls were gored with holes. They entered the shack. Simon was surprised to see a kitchen filled not with cooking equipment, but with a city of machines: towering monitors, sprawling mixing boards, and roads of recording tape weaving through bumpers and reels, all powered by a fridge-sized generator. A hot plate and a few books shared the bedside table with a jointed desk lamp that hung like an inquisitive insect over the bed where an impressive figure lay, arms crossed behind its head. The man rose to greet them, furry dreadlocks dripping around his face. No one introduced him, but Simon heard Nat call the man Spider.

David and Nat placed the electronic keyboard, David's drum, and the guitar in the centre of the room and started to assemble a playing area, all without talk or noise. Spider put a kettle on the hot plate and sprinkled jasmine leaves into a tea-pot.

"So, what does he play?" he asked David, pointing his chin toward Simon.

"Cricket," David said, smiling maliciously. The other two chuckled. "But he so sweeeet, I think he want to mostly play with dolls." They laughed. Simon left the house.

The beach was tiny. The coarse, white sand sparkled, tittering, sharing the joke at his expense. He walked along the foot of the cliff to the far side of the beach. Encompassed by the sea in front and the cliffs that curved behind him, Simon felt a wonderful loneliness and watched the surf crash against the cradling rocks of the lagoon. Returning to the centre of the beach, he wondered what to do. Noises of tuning and "test, test, one two three," came from the house. He decided he would continue practising, so he ran up the dirt path, retrieved his bat from the car, and ran back down to the beach as a warm up for his training session.

He placed an invisible wicket at one end of the beach,

assembled the players, put the umpire in place, listened for the murmurings of the spectators, called out "play!" and waited for the bowler to deliver his ball. He played the first inning as the best batsman for the West Indies.

Music poured out of the shack, with feedback occasionally ringing out in the cliffs. Simon grew bored with his game and decided to cool off in the sea, careful not to go too deep into the surf, aware of the dangers of the undertow. The frothing waves tugged him out gently as they waned. The sky was clear, vast, its only perimeter the sea. He stared, with his head thrown back, almost dizzy in the surf. Out of nowhere, it seemed, a flock of birds came into view. They circled above the cliff behind him and then, slowly descending, flew out above the surf. Large brown birds with white splashes on the head and neck, and large pointed, broad beaks. One of them circled just above him, tucked in its wings, pointed its head down, and dropped through the air in what seemed a noble, suicidal dive. It hit the water, then quickly resurfaced, smacking its beak, swallowing fish. Pelicans. He had never seen pelicans in Barbados before. The only ones he'd ever seen were in the zoo in Guyana, where they'd paddled about at the bottom of a cage. This pelican flock circled above him. Soon, another bird dived. Still another, and another, and another, until they were all plunging before him like sleek missiles dropped from a bomber. But these missiles recouped the air and spiralled back through its invisible currents, up to the height of the cliff where their motion became imperceptible. Perched on the air, they rested before the next dive. A few minutes later, the feeding continued.

Simon stood transfixed, the sea breaking at his waist. He could hear David singing in the distance: "*Don't cry . . . comin' back to find you . . . don't cry love . . .*" It was a drizzly moan, with vowels winding over a reggae beat, breaking up and coming together again: *do on' cryee ee luu uuv.* He'd never heard such a beautiful sound. And dive after dive the pelicans continued their assault from heaven. The hair rose on Simon's arms. He blushed, the flow rising from his waist up to his ears. On the edge of that moment he could feel all the potential of the world.

His brother was weaving a veil of notes, interlacing sounds from each corner of the world into a web where there was just his voice and the word "cry"—repeated like onomatopoeia—a sound caught like a dying fly. In that moment, in the trapped corner of a word, David was defined for Simon. Music had chosen him and nothing else could tempt him. Simon envied that claiming, and he bristled with the need to define himself with the same power he heard in David's voice, a power that sang from a perspective far beyond his own. While Simon had fixated on the movement of muscle and the composition of the perfect play, David was hearing the ripples of the universe. How could he, Simon, put his talents to use in the world, how could he combine the perfect maths scores he was getting at school with the physical sensations he experienced playing cricket, standing in the ocean, or just staring at the sky? He wanted to understand the orchestration of elements that conspired to produce such small, intense, happy moments.

He stood in the surf, watching as the bombarding pelicans gorged themselves until one by one they disappeared out to sea.

The drive home was peaceful and mostly silent, except for a brave moment near Sam Lord's Castle when from the back seat Simon told Nat and David that he had seen pelicans. The two laughed in disbelief.

"Too many cricket balls been hittin' your head, boy," Nat teased. "There aren't pelicans in Barbados anymore, not since they filled in the sea between Pelican Island and Barbados itself, not since the bulldozers levelled the causeway," he assured Simon, who kept his thoughts to himself for the rest of the drive home. He stared out at the passing cane fields, but his eyes kept returning to the back of David's dark head.

At the end of the school term Simon could feel something

ominous in the atmosphere at Willowdale. Mackenzie's sermons became a mix of Genesis and Psalms, hopeful yet foreboding. Simon twice caught David in secret telephone conversations, mentioning dates and dollar figures that didn't seem connected to school. He saw David checking the mailbox daily before MacKenzie could get to it, and realised something serious was afoot.

One day toward the end of June, as he was leaving the house, he encountered David walking up the drive from the mailbox carrying two letters. David's face was serious, not as usual on the verge of grinning. Simon stopped in front of him and summoned his courage to stand firm and expectant, but this time his silent presence had no effect. David walked around his brother and headed solemnly into the house. It wasn't until that evening, when they were seated at the table for dinner, that Simon understood. Edwin had shut himself away with David in the living room. The low tones of their conversation edged higher and higher, until the sudden, grating, "Ingrate! . . . Thankless, unmindful, selfish . . ." exploded into the evening.

The tree frogs, cicadas, and even the barking watchdogs down the road that routinely tuned up as the sun dropped went silent, interrupted by Edwin's cry. His voice broke off, as if he'd realised that words could not be damaging enough. The rest of the family picked at their dinner in silence. The exam results, mailed from England, revealed David had failed, disqualifying him from either of his father's choices for his future and securing his own.

Edwin retreated to the library, where he stayed the remainder of the evening. David walked out of the living room with a confident strut, sat down, and ate quickly and heartily, ignoring the hush around the table. Pushing back his chair, he announced that he was going to visit Nat. Grace rose and moved quickly to the door, blocking his way. Simon noted that David was now considerably taller than their mother. Even so, her long confident frame stopped him.

"What is it that you think you're doing?"

Grace was usually able to make David confide in her, but he avoided her eyes and looked back to the faces at the table, all staring at him, mouths suspended in mid-chew. He looked at the floor and shifted his weight.

"I'm going to rehearse," he said.

"And then what are you going to do?"

David hesitated. Simon's stomach clenched, waiting for the unpredictable.

"I already told Dad, I can borrow the money."

Simon looked to Francie who seemed to be equally in the dark. When he looked back at Grace he saw her right foot rise, hesitate, then fall again to the floor, where it stamped the wood gently. Her imposing glare turned anxious; she shook her head and moved out of the way to let David pass.

MacKenzie started to clear the table, taking up even Maggie's unfinished plate of okra and fish, giving Maggie reprieve from the one vegetable she loathed. As she stood at the kitchen sink washing dishes, MacKenzie began to sing.

"When you walk through a storm
hold your head up high,
and don't be afraid of the dark.
At the end of the storm
is a golden light
and the sweet silver song of a lark."

Francie plugged her ears and went into her bedroom, Maggie skipped off to play with her miniatures in the living room, and Grace joined Edwin in the library, leaving Simon alone at the table as he slipped into the crack in MacKenzie's voice, wondering what a lark looked like.

The next morning, Edwin had already left for the clinic by

the time the family was waking, taking turns in the bathroom. David and Simon arrived simultaneously at the kitchen table. MacKenzie was preparing toast. On the table was a large envelope addressed to David. As he slit it open an object that had been folded up inside unwound and popped out, startling him. David took it from the envelope: a long reed, golden except at the tip where two inches of deep red stained the grain like acid on litmus paper. Simon and David both recognised the bristle from a broom. David's blood. At the time, neither of them paused to wonder why their father would have kept such a thing—the straw that had driven him out of his native country.

David placed the straw on the table and unfolded the accompanying note, which Simon read over his arm:

> *Some journeys are like anchors, inviting you to sink.*
> *Do what you have to do.*
> > > > *Dad.*

Two weeks later, David left for New York. After the arrival of the letter, the colour and bounty seemed to drain out of Willowdale. The usual lively discussions at suppertime had grown muted—but Simon found out about David's departure just two days before the flight. He arrived home with his friend Phillip after digging for sand dollars at low tide near the reef at Sandy Beach.

The two boys had believed they would earn their fortune selling the sand dollars to tourists. In those days, vendors roamed the beaches peddling handmade jewellery out of briefcases. The coral reefs were alive, the coral jewellery trade just beginning. Barbados was the blossom of the Caribbean, a tropical little England charmingly suspended in time. Simon knew boys at school who would dive weekly to harvest branches of coral, carve and polish them into shapely pieces, and sell them for high prices on the beach. But that day Simon and Phillip had collected mostly broken, worthless sea trinkets by the time they got hungry and packed it in. When he arrived in the Garden, towed on the seat of Phillip's bicycle, Simon's calves were stiff from holding tight to the frame while balancing the fragments of sand dollars, sea spiders, and useless shells in the bag slung over his right shoulder.

Opening the gate to their house, Simon saw his mother crouched over a cloth spread out on sheets under the carport canopy. The material was fine wool, the finest worsted pinstripe he had ever seen, except in photographs of visiting foreigners, some of them royalty, who had arrived in Barbados wearing dark, northern armour. He bent to examine the cloth and could smell the weave as though the fabric had been spun that morning, the scent of friction still on its fibres.

"Wha' dis?" he asked his mother who unfolded the last edge.

"It's a suit—it will be a suit—for your brother. He's going to New York."

"What?"

"Not what. Where. New York."

Simon paused to consider what it was exactly that she was telling him. His heart began to race.

"But mummy, no one meks a whole suit from scratch now-a-days."

She looked up at him with annoyance from between her rounded shoulders, her almond eyes almost disappearing into her cheeks.

"Simon, go into the house and bring me the straight pins from my machine bureau."

"But mummy, what's goin' on?"

Grace's focus was unshakable as she carefully laid the pattern on the wool. Simon obediently headed inside.

"The Dragon ain' gon like dis," Phillip whispered to him.

Phillip was referring to Simon's father. Simon shrugged.

Phillip was fascinated by Chinese astrology and had charted the Carter family, telling both Simon and Edwin, born in years of the Dragon, that they were special: "The world is hard for you, 'cause you're its best invention: Impossible. Very sensitive, but don't like to be challenged. You know how hard it is to be a child, but there's no disguising who's the boss." Simon was born in a Water Dragon year, and was a February child, a placid Pisces. Phillip reserved the sobriquet of The Dragon for Edwin, an Earth Dragon and a Leo, signs that made him a force to contend with.

Phillip wiped his hand across his smile to produce a frown, pointed to himself, and then, breast-stroking in the air, moved to his bicycle, not wanting to witness The Dragon's arrival. Simon passed the bag to his friend and whispered that he'd meet him later, then entered the house to search his mother's sewing room. No, The Dragon was not going to like this.

On his way back with the straight pins, Simon met up with MacKenzie, who was carrying a tray with a pitcher of lime squash and a glass full of ice.

"If fire drop 'pon yuh an' yuh chile, who yuh 'gin brush it offa first?" she said, looking at Simon but not expecting an answer. Pushing the door open with her shoulder, she took the lime squash to his mother.

That evening the suit was cut. David didn't appear for dinner, but Simon heard him sneaking in, trying to tread softly across the floor, long after everyone, except his mother, was in bed. The sound of her sewing machine had kept Simon awake. On the edge of sleep in the early morning, when even the tree frogs had stopped singing, Simon thought the clip and sew noises from the back of the house had ceased. But when he woke at six she was at it again, continuing all the next day and through the night before David left.

Simon and his sisters convened in Best's work shed at the side of the house to share what information they had gleaned from overheard conversations or the occasional answers to their questions.

"David said he was goin' no matter what," Francie declared breathlessly, swept up in the excitement of events that always surrounded her older brother. "Daddy decided to give him the money at the last minute, only after he made David promise to study there, take music lessons. But David told me he won' take any lessons, he's got a friend who'll hire him straight into a band."

"But he doesn't know anyone in New York!"said Simon, inventing obstacles that might magically stop David from setting their whole world off balance.

"No, but Spider does, and that's who he's goin' with," said Francie. Simon bristled at the fact that Francie should know this, when it was he who had met Spider and heard their music, but then Francie and David had always confided more easily than the two brothers.

Maggie began to cry.

"He'll come back soon," Simon said feebly.

"I shouldn't have taken them."

"What are you talkin' about?" he asked.

"His best agates and steelies . . . I shouldn't have taken them."

"It's alright. David doesn't use those baby things anymore, Mags," Francie said.

"No, you're wrong. He would, they're special," Maggie continued, convinced of something Simon could not grasp. "When I was sneakin' them back to his room last night he caught me, and he said I could keep them 'cause he didn't need them now, 'cause where he was going people would really know who he is, and that we don't. Not one of us."

Simon felt an angry twitch in his groin. David's knottiness always affected the rest of them, and yet Simon had under-estimated the significance of his brother's visit to Ragged Point and the bewitching sounds that had come from the shack. He pushed back the curls from Maggie's eyes, fighting his own tears. When he heard sniffles from Francie he knew he couldn't give in to the sadness; he would have to set the example for all of them.

As they were beginning dinner the night before David's departure, Edwin tapped his glass with a knife to get the family's attention. He raised the glass of rum above his head in a toast: "Your brother is to become a star, one we'll miss in this hemisphere, of course: he'll be a northern star."

Simon heard the tired lash of fear in his father's voice and was embarrassed for him. His eyes darted around the room. Francie rubbed David's arm proudly, as David calmly chewed his food, his face betraying nothing beyond what Simon had heard by the cliffs: the resolute claim that music had made on his brother. Grace refilled David's glass with lemonade and offered him seconds from the plate of fish. She caught sight of Edwin's pained smile. She grinned back and held out the plate in his direction. Edwin declined, but Maggie speared a piece. Grace smoothed back Maggie's hair as she watched her eat, and then looked down at her own plate and cut another slice of fish, grasping at the threads of their unravelling family tapestry. Simon found it difficult to swallow.

At the airport the next day, Francie created a scene with her wailing. To calm her, David rubbed her shoulders, and she nestled into his arms. After she had quieted, David got up to stretch his legs and strutted purposefully around the airport in the new suit that rushed him northward, into maturity. He sweated in the jacket and starched white shirt that set off the faint stripes in the wool, but he kept the jacket on for his mother's sake. She occasionally patted the collar or felt along the hem of the sleeves as though seeing stitches she'd missed in the dark. By then, her eyes were inky slivered almonds. When

David finally walked through the "passengers only" barrier, Grace could only smile feebly, too exhausted to be sad. He disappeared.

At first Grace received regular letters from David, in which he described the Bronx and the trips into Manhattan to see famous bands. The letters petered out and eventually stopped. Grace's letters to him were returned unopened, with "Addressee Unknown" stamped across them. When she finally heard from him again she was relieved, but these new letters were sent without a return address, said nothing about David's activities, containing only extensive anecdotes and musings on how people cope with living in the cold. It wasn't until years later that any of the family saw him again.

Simon is stiff and cold, his joints restless with sitting. He gets up and walks around the basement to rush the warmth to his feet. He can't hear anything from upstairs—*what is she doing?* A pile of magazines and newspapers on his desk—geographical society magazines, earth science journals—reminds him of all the reading he has promised himself to undertake. If his job at the Ministry of Natural Resources is eliminated, he will be able to catch up, to reclaim the parts of himself absent since the years of generalisation. Flat representations of the earth's surface with landscape features described by symbols, all maps are generalisations. A map cannot portray reality: detail is lost at the reduced scale. *I long for release from simplification, smoothing, displacement, and classification.*

He extends his arms up to the ceiling, stretching his tightened muscles, releasing his joints. Up, up onto his toes, stretching high, higher . . . then release. Blood to his extremities flows with memory.

Simon's life at home without David was different in the way a snake is different after shedding its first skin—bigger, brighter coloured, but more menacing and dangerous. The first evening his parents went out and left Simon in charge of his sisters and the house the rush of power was palpable. He told Francie to get off the phone and stop tying up the line. Even though Francie was older, she accepted the traditional line of command and made a quick excuse to her friend, saying she'd call back later. When he tucked Maggie into bed and told her to "sleep tight don' let the bedbugs bite," his step out of the darkened room was proud and full of purpose; he wanted to run with this new strength. Where would he put this feeling?

He took driving lessons, and when he got his licence it became his duty to take Maggie to her swimming lessons after school and to drop Francie off at her friends' on Rendezvous Ridge, pick her up, and on occasion chaperon her to dances. Phillip accompanied him, a silent but animated navigator in the passenger seat. But errands and duties licked up their time and the novelty of power soon wore off.

Phillip wanted to become a performer, and, after having seen Marcel Marceau once on television, a mime artist. A boy known for his theatrical gestures, he had eyebrows that could glide across his forehead. His mouth was ordinary when closed, but he could make it resemble the long tunnel into the stalactite caverns of Harrison's cave, or transform his tongue into the beak of a bird. Phillip was unusual in any setting, but on the tiny island his oddness was conspicuous.

Their dreamy days spent together on the beach became less frequent. Once, after snorkelling for sand dollars for most of the day, Phillip built himself a circle of sand, ceremoniously placed a coconut at its centre, and proceeded to transform himself into two characters. One man had Phillip's big lips, fleshy nose, and round face; the other a sucking-on-lemon look, with cheeks pulled in and lips puckered. A group of tourists congregated, watching him with timid curiosity. The round-faced man moved like Marceau, lithely, gracefully. He sang a silent song while strumming an invisible guitar. He finished his song after having casually rested one foot on top of the coconut. The sour-faced man marched to the centre of the circle to confront the other. They proceeded to have a conversation about the fruit on the ground. The crowd grew larger. Simon lost his view of the performance because so many had gathered on the beach, but there was laughter and then applause. When Phillip was finished and the crowd had dispersed, Simon asked him what his performance had been about. Reluctant to speak, Phillip mumbled, "Consolation," and walked away.

That word festers. *Whose?*

The afternoon in the basement wanes. Simon misses the innocent wisdom of Phillip's face—the only face that could make him laugh as he became increasingly serious and studious. After David's departure, Edwin took greater interest in Simon's schooling and, seduced by The Dragon's encouragement, Simon became a model student. Even in the summer he would study books on geology, chemistry, and physics brought home from the library. His interests settled on earth sciences, finding his first puzzles in MacKenzie's obsession with salt. She continued to bless and curse the family through her chant and encouraged Simon's interest, while damning the analytical approach inherited from his father.

"Hol' de light fuh de devil to see an' when yuh get a chance, blow it out in 'e face," she recommended. She showed Simon how to prepare saltfish and how to serve it with ackee—not the sweet creamy fruit Bajans sucked on but a yellow fleshy egg-like fruit that came in cans from Jamaica, which her cousin sent regularly by post from Kingston. The fish was garnished with prayer:

"This salt, O Lord, may you sanctify by your power of sanctification and may you bless it with your blessing, so that it may become a perfect medicinal for all who receive it and may remain in every fibre of their being. In the name of our Lord

Jesus Christ, who will come to judge the living and the dead and the world by fire. Amen."

Like his father, Simon scorned her superstition and went to the library for the truth. There he discovered the complexity of the crystalline compound now taken for granted as something merely to be avoided in a healthy diet. But for many thousands of years human beings longed for salt and travelled, fought, built, and destroyed over it. Salt was once the booty of ancient battles for territory, and the commodity upon which new trading centres were established throughout Europe. Salt was currency. It was a marker of civilisation. In the pre-Christian millennium salt was used in cleaning, bleaching, and dyeing fabrics, degreasing, dehairing, and softening leather, and in almost any operation where a chemical reaction was required. It was used later in the preservation of precious fish, meat, and other food. The quest for salt became a quest for sophistication. Saltworks became an institution. As Simon learned, but didn't mention to MacKenzie, salt and ecclesiastical interests were tightly associated, and sources of salt often determined the location of monasteries. Salt was the driving force behind the building of some of Europe's earliest roads and cities. Whole military campaigns were waged for sources of salt.

And where there was industry, there was taxation. Salt was a commodity in universal demand, its supply not left to chance. Easier than most other necessities to control, and as its consumption was directly related to population, salt was an appropriate base for taxation. Monopolies became a significant problem both in Europe and China. Governments tried to control salt production and distribution and to derive revenue from its sale. Since the sovereign had traditionally owned the "fruits of the earth," then salt was arguably his as well. He could maintain a complete monopoly, from production to the sale of salt. The organisation of this monopoly was, however, almost impossible for any government to maintain, and led to smuggling and private production. Not only was the salt tax the most hated of all taxes in Europe during the eighteenth century, it is speculated to have been a major cause of the French Revolution.

Simon was not as interested in the salt industry as he was in its sources. He learned that salt is remarkably well-distributed over the globe and is rarely lacking in any area of considerable size. First, there is the sea. Bounteous. Inland brine springs also provide it. From both these sources either solar evaporation or boiling is crucial to production. Where sea water or brine is evaporated, all of the contained salts precipitate out. The main constituent salt, which separates from the others, is sodium chloride. Pure sodium chloride can be found in the salt beds left behind by ancient seas or lining the shores of seas in the process of drying up—a commonplace desert phenomenon. Salt from these salt beds is rocklike and has been used as a building material: in the nineteenth century explorers found houses constructed of rock salt in Saharan Africa. To Simon's fascination he discovered that deeper within the earth lie salt deposits that have been forming for over five-hundred million years. Upon reaching the surface of the earth they are mined. In modern times, even the vast underground deposits that do not extend to the surface are mined, producing industrial salt.

"Industrial salt is washed. It loses its flavour; it tastes metallic," he read in an interview with a French woman from Guerande where they still practise the ancient method of obtaining salt from the sea. In Guerande a whole a new generation of salt makers has revived the dying trade of sea salt and, along with producers of foie gras, mustard, and wine, have returned salt to a culinary luxury. "Natural sea salt is pure," the woman continues. "It is low in sodium but rich in minerals like magnesium, potassium, and zinc. Its benefits to the body are manifold."

Simon turned to yet another book that examined the

mysteries of salt. Salt is edible rock, yet it dissolves completely in water. It preserves but also corrodes. We are salty because life began in the sea, but the earth is full of salt that has no trace of marine life. Our bodies crave salt, but eating it causes thirst. Simon's skin tingled. These contradictions made his physical activities seem even more profound. After sweating from a robust cricket match, he would lick his lips, his hands, his shoulders, in awe of the ingenuity that had sucked this sensation from skin and sprinkled it on food, replenishing the body's supply. The earth was a body producing salt, just like his own body. We could make the earth sweat, we could taste its soul.

The ancient method of obtaining salt involves channelling sea water into shallow ditches dug into the ground. The inflow is shut off during the hot season, the water evaporates from the ground, and leaves a crust of salt deposited in the channel. The salt crystals are scooped off the earth like a delicate film of ice. One day Simon set up his own experiment. He built a wooden trough from old planks in Best's work shed. Onto the trough he fixed a piece of slate from the remnants of a countertop. The slate formed a barrier that could be slid in and out of the front of the trough. He took his materials, along with a sharp spade, to the beach. Near the rocks at the eastern extremity of Accra Beach he dug a channel in the sand that would allow sea water to enter at high tide. He fixed the trough in place and waited until the tide forced a sufficient amount of water into the trough. He slid down the slate barrier and went home. He returned the next day to keep track of the evaporation. It worked. The day after, the water-level was lower still; he could scrape crystals from around the inflow line of the trough. Magic: he was making salt.

While preoccupied with geology, Simon was not oblivious to biology. His fixation on his own changing body as a young boy had expanded to include the female body—breasts, organs, and the touch and smell of skin.

Edith. Simon can see her pocked and oily skin amidst the decorated faces of Francie's friends. Her eyes nestle deeply under the ridge of her bumpy brow and her rare smile reveals crooked teeth. Her coarse black hair spreads out over her head like a crowded coral sea fan that she pins behind her ears, but which is always escaping, and so she has developed the unappealing tick of caressing behind her ear. Edith was whisper-whisper ugly—no one saying it aloud, all agreeing.

Simon and Phillip had been required as chaperones for a dance at Windward on Old Year's Night. At the beginning of the evening, before they got into his Austin Epic, Phillip had looked over at Simon, stuck out his chest, and gestured with his hands that he was on the lookout for large, round, smooth breasts that night. He placed phantom breasts in his mouth and closed his eyes, his face dreamy and quenched. Simon blushed, but confessed the same desire over the roof of the car.

Phillip was a champion with girls because he was an excellent dancer. Girls who weren't intimidated by his exaggerated expressions, mobile eyebrows, and the matted mane he'd recently decided to grow into dreadlocks, would flock around him, hoping to be his partner, the one he would float with to a silent plane where love was in the slightest sway of a hip. It was easy for Simon to meet girls with Phillip as his best friend, but he rarely took advantage of the opportunities.

As the countdown to midnight began, Simon found himself face to face with Edith who until then had remained shyly at the back of the pack of girls surrounding Phillip. After the *5, 4, 3, 2, 1, Happy New Year!*, she took his head between her hands and gave him a friendly smack on the lips. Then she took his hand and led him to the dance floor where she began to gyrate and bounce, and was transformed. Her face and twiny hair disappeared, and she became her fleshy curves, enslaving Simon. When he put his arms around her waist, his elbows could rest on her hips. They danced until the sun came up, she with her

eyes closed, drooping about his neck, he with a hard bulge in
his trousers. But the closest he came to her breasts was when
she pressed them against him during long, slow songs. The scent
of her musk fogged his brain, and he was sure he could feel
erect nipples through her satin dress.

Six months later he touched her breasts for the first time.
Edith was slow and careful, like a panther, arriving at the moment
of lust as though it were a kill. When she finally let him touch
the skin inside her thighs she was ravenous and came on his
hand, crying "shit, oh shit." After that she began to reveal herself
to him quickly: we are all forms of God, she told him; she
believed in reincarnation, and in this life she was learning
forbearance. In her next life, she chimed as they rolled together
on the floor of her father's work shed, she'd come back to earth
as a mongoose and her lesson would be shrewdness. As Simon
licked and sucked all the precious folds of her body, she
hummed the Merrymen's calypso "Sly Mongoose." She was
both a vessel and its contents, pouring in and out of herself at
various moments, sometimes full, sometimes drained. When
Simon first met Faye, he was reminded of Edith in the way a
riddle could be hidden in Faye's every carefully considered word.

Before Simon left for university in Canada, he and Edith
discussed their futures, with painful avoidance on his part of an
eventual union. But one day she said to him: "I'll cook and
clean for you, but I'll never look after you." He didn't understand what she meant. He had never until then considered the
domestic scene she was describing. But when he met Faye he
instantly understood the difference between duty and care. He
was as delicate with Faye as he was vulnerable to her. They
took, they gave, they trusted. Family. But . . .

It's getting dark. The sun's life is short these days and by
eight o'clock he begins to feel sleepy. Their usual dinner hour
has come and gone, and there is no rumble of hunger in his
belly, but he hears movement in the kitchen. He will go up. She

is preparing food. Duty or care? If only we always knew the truth. *If I could take her hand from the pot and plunge it into my soul I would.*

Faye watches Simon sitting at the kitchen table, staring down at his food, holding his fork without purpose. *Eat! Eat!* she wants to shout . . . . *chew, chew, chew* . . . . but he pushes a few morsels of pasta around on the plate and then gulps water from his glass. She watches his face while nibbling from her own plate.

He looks like a phantom—hollow eyes, yellow where they should be white. She knows he is doing his best. Is he somewhere in the past, reconstructing conversations with David—perhaps their final meeting, perhaps the days before their break—a way to recoup his own innocence? *Why is it that we all feel guilty?* She wonders if that might be what David wanted. Is this punishment? Was his suicide a supreme act of selfishness, or just a spit in the eye of despair?

She used to think that her mother's nervous breakdown was a coward's way of living, but she's come to understand it as strong and creative, a means of leaving the world without having to tie a noose, wield a razor blade, gag on pills. And yet to prepare a noose as effectively as David had, requires physical dexterity and consciousness that defies obliteration; it almost reinforces a worldly existence.

"Do you imagine that at any moment he hesitated?" she asks Simon, having found out more of the story today, but not knowing how much he knows. She watches as his pasta loses its heat and becomes a cold gluey mass of starch.

"Have you spent time wondering that?" he asks finally.

She has said the wrong thing again—*shit, stupid, stupid* . . . treading on forbidden turf, the sacred territory of the inexplicable, the realm of speculation. She searches for something else to say but can see it's futile. She clears the dishes and begins to run water in the sink.

"Let me do those," he offers politely.

"No, really, I don't mind. It gives me something to do; I don't feel like practising, and it's early. Please." She lies. *Turn the dishes oooover.* She watches Simon turn and shuffle through the living room toward the basement. He disappears down the stairs.

She presses the search button on the stereo to skip to the next disc. Dvorak. Piano Quintet. She loves this music, especially the opening A major allegro, where the cello holds the melody. She would like to be practising. It's the only thing that gives her relief from this last week, and tomorrow she has to return to her cubicle to sell more subscriptions. Her poor sales recently have her thinking about taking a different approach. Would wealthy matrons respond better to grief? If she could translate the weight of grief in this house, the frivolous sound of art might instead become *aaauugghhhrrrtttt* and would more precisely convey the agony and sublimity of notes, metaphors, brushstrokes. She will experiment.

She finishes the dishes and returns to her studio. Dvorak is in his scherzo, a Bohemian dance. It is direct and joyful. She finds comfort in its message. Faye and Michael used to argue about music. She loved what the piece said, and he loved how it was said. He enjoyed music that was indirect and formal, and was happy when he spent a month rehearsing the orchestra for *Die Zauberflote*, because of its strange, secretive Masonic ethos. The libretto's allusions were to secrets of the Masonic brothers for whom Schikaneder had written it. The secrets confounded Faye, and she learned that she'd never be privy to their sacraments. She felt for Papageno, who would not exchange the tangible material world for the vague promise of an ideal one. She was left wondering why the Queen of the Night didn't take up the magic flute herself to prevent her daughter's abduction, when even the foreign prince, Tamino, could master it on his first try. The Queen of the Night, the embodiment of the negative principle, is introduced in G-minor, the bereft mother. She promises her daughter to the hero, but in the same aria she has a sudden and complete transformation into a tenacious demon. By the second act she is the larger-than-life villain in D-minor and gives her daughter away. Her most famous aria has her sounding like a clucking, pecking, hysterical bird. Faye listened to her, night after night in the pit, under the influence of the treatment she was receiving at the fertility clinic. The arias dislodged her, she was hurled into fever. One night she almost collapsed, had to stop playing. Michael threw her a ministerial glare from his podium. They had a terrible fight that night when they got home, and Michael found a subtle way to remind her that she was in the orchestra only due to his influence.

And Nannerl's opera? Faye is certain Nannerl would never have allowed arbitrary characters to represent abstract principles. A sorority like the Masons? Would its secrets have required reci-tatives for domestic battles, requia for the frequent death of a young child? Wolfgang's first son died at two months, unsung. Or would there be, perhaps, an aria buffa for the drudgery of dishes?

Faye had thrown a cup at Michael. She said she wanted to stop the fertility treatment, to try something else, to try adoption. Michael attempted to calm her down, but she was not to be mollified. He said that if the problems were chemical they needed chemical solutions. After all, she had been the one who wanted a child. She threw a plate. He said they could go to a different clinic. She hurled a glass and it hit the wall just missing his head. Then remorse. *Sorry, sorry, oh shit, oh sorry.* Later she acquiesced. Of course, he was right; it was logical, so logical. She continued the treatment.

Today she is ovulating. She can feel it, knowing the small signs so well. She feels she should be like the Queen of the Night, the bereft mother, cackling her way through the day— *pa pa pa pa . . . pa pa pa pa*—releasing the tension of hope. She waits for the dizziness, but it doesn't come. Just Dvorak's cello, peacefully mapping out a simple, light path to something else.

Did David have second thoughts? Faye's question sticks with Simon. Her magic is curious, presenting riddles, bringing flecks of possibility shimmering to the surface that he must mine. She has always known more about David—knowledge that is suspended between them like a bridge. Upstairs, he wanted to acknowledge her efforts to look after him, to comfort him, and he is ashamed of his silence. He goes to the bookcase and begins to rub the sandpaper lightly over the pine again.

The uncertainty that Faye has suggested in David's death— surely an impossibility. Everything that David did was so calculated and wilful. Nothing in his life seemed to happen outside his immense control, so why should his death be any different? His will seemed to overpower everyone else's.

Simon rubs and rubs the wood.

The year before David left for New York, their father was asked to go to Brazil as part of a team to help control a crippling outbreak of swine fever. He was to be away for three weeks, and Grace, who had never really taken to Barbados and longed for some continental life, decided to go with him. The four children were left in the charge of MacKenzie, who was to make sure they ate properly, went to bed at usual hours. Most of all, she was to ensure that Edwin's car stayed parked in the driveway. Fussy with the new Ford, Edwin would let David drive it only if he accompanied him. When the taxi came to take them to the airport, Edwin gave MacKenzie the keys, which Simon saw her put into the pocket of her shift.

A few hours after their parents had left, David called to his brother and sisters: "Hey, ya'll come, we gon' for a ride."

Francie yelped with joy, ran to the car and waited by the passenger door. Maggie started to cry. MacKenzie and Simon stared at David in disbelief.

"Now, don' look pon' me so, woman," he taunted, and then dangled the keys in front of MacKenzie's moist, shining face.

"How in God's name did you get—" she started and then clutched her empty pocket.

"Don' fuss wid me woman, I ain' gon' to hurt the old man's chooka chooka."

"Masta David, yuh ears hard hard, yuh heard yuh fatha."

David smiled and shouted to the rest: "Get in."

Francie threw herself in happily, but Maggie cuddled up to MacKenzie's thick thigh. David looked at Simon and raised his eyebrows in challenge. Simon stepped stiffly to the car and climbed in the back seat.

"Masta Simon, no, don't. Follow-follow kill monkey. I gon' ask the reverend to pray fo yuh this Sunday, Laud have Mercy."

David got in, grinned his grin, and before the door shut, Simon heard MacKenzie continue, "If yuh head bad, yuh whole body bad."

The three siblings went down the road birdspeed. They spent the day in and out of Bridgetown, in and out of rum shops where David stopped to fire a drink with barmen who knew him. Francie was overjoyed, riding on a romantic wave of defiance. David was impressive but frightening. If he could defy MacKenzie and her duppy curses, he was stronger than Simon had realised. MacKenzie never told Edwin about the incident, probably unwilling to confess her failure in the face of the grinning demon.

To this day, Simon cannot figure out how David took the keys without the servant noticing. He would have had to slip his hand so near her belly as to tickle her. He was a magician, capable of getting in and out of anything. Was his maneuver with the noose a magician's trick gone wrong; did he think he could slip out of its embrace the way he had any tight spot he found himself in? *Was she trying to tell me something I didn't know?* Simon kicks out, frustrated. His foot hits the bookcase and it topples over.

CHAPTER 4

Water

Faye lies on her side, on the floor, her head propped on her hand. Flip, flip, passing time through a fashion magazine. Models pout and pucker, long and lean like her, but without the awkwardness. Born with style? Something about them all is the same: each carries the gene for fashion.

Faye has ogled genetics since her days at the fertility clinic.

They're making sexless pigs in England. Scientists are manipulating the sex chromosomes of fetuses to create androgynous pigs, because it's too expensive to castrate one in today's competitive hog market. *Oink.*

Beneficent goals abound. Ojibwa-Cree in northern Ontario are trading their DNA to scientists for fresh vegetables, and royalties, should a cure for diabetes results from the research. Scientists are targeting mosquitoes for genetic modification, stockpiling ammunition in the global battle against insect-borne disease. Genetically altered, sterile male mosquitoes are released into the world to compete with fertile males for female partners and, thus, reduce the eventual number of offspring. Genetic rather than chemical sterility ensures that males are sterile yet vigorous in their sexual advances. At least they're not deprived of that.

And, of course, there's Dolly. *Dolly, dolly, lamb aaahhh . . . .* little Dolly, the clone of a sheep, half asleep. The first living clone. But you can't clone souls, poor Dolly. Her soul isn't shared with her original source, so, like the rest of us, she's doomed to search for her soul mate. Roaming, roaming the earth, grazing, searching, trying to reconnect . . . waiting and waiting for that moment when eyes lock and *"ah, so it's you, there you are,"* forms on the tongue. We have finally reproduced

Plato's creature: that double-appendaged, two-headed first beast
that, because the gods were angered, was separated into two and
sentenced to roam the planet looking for its other half. Platonic
love . . . *bhaaahhh.*

Nature tricks and can be tricked. A game of reason.
Illusions of cause and effect. Faye was born in the Chinese year
of the Pig. If humans were as fecund as pigs, would we have the
luxury of technology? Big-brained species have to be born one
at a time, and in that way are bestowed the luxury of play, which
experts note is essential to early mental development. But with
fertility drugs, women are giving birth to quints, now octuplets,
born in batches, just like pigs. Bigger brains, bigger batches,
more and more solutions to human problems. But humans have
two significant inheritances: from the Greeks, hubris—retri-
bution for attempts to usurp the power of god; and from the
Hebrews, blasphemy—that ultimate and immanently punishable
offence against Him. We remain bridled heirs to both. But it
took two years of feeling like a laboratory animal at the fertility
clinic before Faye began to sense these legacies.

At first she had been happy with Michael, learning from
him, oblivious to the slow osmosis, the subtle melting of her
own ego. The only obstacle to becoming him seemed to be the
formality of skin and bone separating fluids, yet her blood
needed his heart to keep it flowing rhythmically. She practised
for six hours a day, unfailingly—four in the morning, stopping
for a break to work part-time at a bookstore, and then another
two in the evening. Bach's solo cello concertos. Every day was
an adventure in arpeggios. Each of her muscles confirmed, as
Michael had quoted Nietzsche, that for music it was worth-
while to live on earth. Surely music preceded speech, developed
from mating calls. With each tug at her bow she was secreting
a magical animal musk that would attract Michael and keep
him sniffing for more. She was suspicious of language, of

misconstrued words that might make her sound stupid, so she played. She gave him the role of teacher, presenting for approval her ideas on syncopation or inversion. He would agree or disagree with little effort, feeding her with tidbits to take away with her into her tiny practice room, or he'd hold her tightly, embracing her the way he held all the notes of a symphony inside his arms.

"You're lovely," he would say softly in a voice like a blanket she slid under.

He was always working—teaching, rehearsing with the orchestra, or listening intensely to music in his own studio. When she was away working or visiting her parents or friends, he would find it difficult to concentrate, impossible to get anything done. He needed her beside him, yet when she was there, he was always busy. Inside himself. When they made love, always in the morning, he was absent, wading into her as though she were a cool lake on a hot day; he was dipping for relief.

At breakfast after a morning's tepid coupling, she screwed up her courage:

"Could I audition for the orchestra?" She took a quick sip of her coffee.

"Mmm?" Michael looked up. A crumb of toast was stuck to his top lip, which Faye tried not to notice.

"Do you think I'm good enough?" she continued. For a long time he said nothing; her confidence was being washed away by the rising lull. He took a sip of coffee.

"So that it doesn't seem unfair, you'll have to audition for the concert master. We'll make a third desk."

Had she heard right? *Skip, skip* . . . her heart missed a beat and in she jumped to the ropes of her own fate, praying almost out loud—*oh help*—that she wouldn't trip.

She practised non-stop and barely met with the concert master's approval. The orchestra's repertoire focused on Bach,

Mozart, Haydn, and some Dvorak. Most of the time the ensemble performed as part of a concert series of eighteenth-century music, but occasionally a few members performed chamber concerts, duets, or, very rarely, experimental contemporary music. Faye's playing improved rapidly, but she felt confident only when supported by the other cellists. Michael was forgiving of the bars he knew she merely mimed, and for that she loved him even more. In the mornings she heartily slid him inside her, knowing that on the pill she would be protected from the banal accident of pregnancy that could spoil her career.

In the orchestra she forgot about the moments at home when she wanted to delve into Michael, to seek out the half-glimpsed resolution to the sounds in her head that had been repeated, over and over, since the day she had taken her mother to the hospital. She longed to discover his secret, sometimes feeling like a creature scratching at a window to be let in. He would work hard, and so would she, thinking the secret might lie there. Her right arm became a firm, sinewy weapon. She would tease him into feeling her biceps, goading his seriousness, and challenge him to arm wrestle. *Scratch scratch . . . let me in.* His arms, too, were tight and strong, and he would wrestle to placate her, never letting her win, just keeping her quiet. *What is the sound of muscle?*

One day she found herself wandering around her studio, unable to play. The silence was disconcerting, for fear of the other sounds that might take over and leave her stranded alone in the hum of her mother's fragility, or, worse, her indifference. She sought out Michael, walking up behind him undetected, observing his concentration over a score.

"Let's take a holiday,"she said cheerfully. It took him a few seconds to look up at her as she came in front of him.

"A holiday?"

"Yes, we've both been working non-stop for ages."

"Oh, I don't know . . ."

Faye knew he was hesitant about missing a beat of his work, measured out so precisely. "We could go to Europe, attend some concerts. That would be almost like work anyway."

It took her a few days to convince him, but he finally agreed. She carefully researched their options, and in the first week of July they flew to Florence.

Florence: the quality of the light on stone and cypress, with flaming amber hills in the distance, made Faye want to sing. *Libiamo ne'lieti calici* . . . She could hear Verdi, and she wanted to see, eat, and drink the city in the way a refined courtesan like Voiletta Valery might have. But Michael was more formal in his approach. He studied the sounds of Tuscany as though they were a score he'd been commissioned to conduct. They were on hallowed ground. They visited all the museums in the city, heard concerts in magnificent halls and outdoor theatres, and marked each fountain with the toss of a coin. Everything echoed. Faye's sense of inadequacy grew along with the amplifying sounds of the things she was avoiding. She didn't look like the women there; she was taller, and the way she dressed seemed buffoonish, more like Rigoletto than the frail and tragic Violetta. *Ah fors'è lui che lamina* . . . *For him her longing soul.* She was too big, and that accelerated her shrinking. Michael joined her. As he hunched over an espresso and a concert program at an outdoor cafe, she was forced to examine him in the light of his own idols. He was dwarfy, uncertain, fumbling where he should have been refined and graceful like the liquid Europeans he considered his cousins. That night in the hotel he penetrated her, but this time when she touched him he was fragile and brittle. And he called out her name—an unheard of sound during their love-making—frightening her. She held his head, brushed back his black hair and sought out his eyes. *Now will you let me in?* They were closed. She began to weep.

The next morning she told Michael she needed a more

restful holiday and begged him to take her away from Florence to somewhere more secluded. They arrived on Elba later that afternoon.

Elba, Napoleon's prison, the island of internment. Paradise as punishment—so Latin. With France besieged on all fronts in 1814, his enemies made a point of telling Napoleon that they were against him and him alone. The allies allowed him to flee to Elba, granting him sovereignty there, letting him keep the title of Emperor, offering him two million francs a year and four hundred guards at his service.

Faye had always thought of Napoleon as a perfectionist, someone whose ambition could never be realised. She liked him: a man trying to be more than he had been endowed. Big small man . . . *runt, runt.* Elba seemed an impossible place for him: untameable, too neutral to be conquered. But perhaps to her it would deliver silence.

They rented a car and drove from the ferry, in search of a suitable hotel, but they were all booked at the height of the tourist season. They found a dowdy *pensione* near a beach and stayed there one night, then the next day drove to the far side of the island to find something better. Cloud cover made the island unenchanting as they toured it. Michael had the car radio turned up loud, and he sang Italian pop songs in a false tenor voice. The hair on Faye's neck felt prickly and irritating. She gazed out the window at the holiday homes along the coast that made the island feel like a vast, hollow suburb. Fantasy had escaped. She began to understand why Napoleon had been sent there, or perhaps it was he who had taken something when he left.

Now she wanted to leave, and once again begged Michael to take her somewhere else. Rome. Rome would have the right sounds. Michael grew impatient with her, raising his voice and, although agreeing that Elba was not ideal, stating emphatically that he wanted time to rest and read. Faye persisted, giving him

dozens of reasons why Rome would suit him and help his work. When they got back to their hotel, they parked the car on the road and called the airline, booked a flight. After a fine dinner of grilled sardines and squid, with more Chianti than she'd ever had before or has had since, they folded up in bed, covered by a single sheet, and slept until the next morning.

They were slow getting started that Sunday, taking their time to have breakfast in the hotel, packing their bags, checking out at noon. They strolled out happy and rested to the car.

Suddenly: feathered and skinned geese, ducks, capons; beans, spinach, collard, rapini; lamb, mutton, goat; tomatoes upon rows of tomatoes. And most prominently: cheese.

Reggiano, Reggiano . . . Provolone, Fontina . . . One vendor's recitatif, while others sang: *Bel Paese, Gorganzola, Domaci Beli Sir . . .*

Their car was buried. They were in the market. Or rather, the market had arrived upon their rented Audi, surrounding it, blocking all paths to or away. Dozens of parked vans, wheels on the sidewalk, had doors opening into stalls of produce. Shoppers squeezed through the lane. Michael's brow creased. Faye heard him exhale—*B-flat?*—as he ran to the stall that jutted from the hood of their car. He tried to find a way to speak to the vendor, to ask him in mime to somehow move the hundreds of pounds of meat that would release their car, release them from Elba. But no Italian emerged from his gestures and Faye was no help. He then gestured in pleading—didn't work—then in anger, demanding the vendor move his van ahead just a little, take down only part of his stall, and let them leave. The vendor shrugged his shoulders, suppressing a vulgar gesture with his hand, and pointed toward the street sign warning motorists of the market each Sunday. Michael stood, helpless, with Faye behind him taking in everything around her. The smells and sounds were swelling. She smelled the people who pushed by her. Voices flowed loudly and quickly and, scrambled with the Chianti of the night before, came sounds from within her. *Turn*

the dishes ooooover . . . She was enticed by the friction of existence.

She imagined Napoleon riding across Elba, darkly tanned for the first time in his life, allowing his shirt to flap unbuttoned in the cooling onshore breeze, rolling up his sleeves to reveal stunted, brown, hairless arms. She turned to Michael, who had started to take crates off the hood of the car, while the vendor spewed curses at him, calling other vendors to help stop this violation. Michael backed down. He put their luggage in the trunk. (Napoleon galloped, the hair usually pulled across his balding brow now flapping wildly.) She could feel Michael's frustration. He grabbed her by the arm to pull her out of the rush of people, but she resisted, wanting to stay. He frowned, but she didn't want to let go of the storm of sensation that opened her and roused what was lacking between the two of them. Michael turned to walk away. (Napoleon slowed to a canter.) She reached to clutch his sleeve, and walked away with him, mustering the effort to calm him, telling him they'd catch the flight the next day.

They decided to spend the afternoon in the sun, to beg space from the sprawling territory of families on the beach in front of the hotel. They needed to wear out the day. (Napoleon retreated for siesta.)

Michael drove the stake of the beach umbrella into the sand then carefully spread a blanket beneath. Faye lay on the sand and exposed her slender tummy to the sun. Time passed slowly in the heat. Michael read a book while she ladled handfuls of sand again and again. She walked to the shore, dipped her toes in the water, but decided against a swim. She sat back down, propped up on her elbows, and observed the families on the beach.

Children buzzed about, their sporty little bodies kicking up sand, building, building, building cities of sand, then other children arriving to smash the dainty castles. Tears. Wailing. Mothers consoling. Faye was fixated by this opera *miniatura*. The

persistent sound of one child's wailing was like the base note beneath the scene. Mothers fed, fussed, refereed, kissed, scolded, kissed more. Mothers were the sentinels of those miniature cities, watching, watching, with never a moment to disappear into themselves—a luxury Faye had always taken for granted. Not only the mothers but the children were never allowed to sink deeply into themselves. She saw that even the outsiders among the children were eventually gathered in, given jobs at castle building, a role in the sand cities. Being in a family meant being surrounded, watched, not allowed to be left loose and wagging off to the side. She felt herself suddenly like frayed cloth, a drooping hem.

The wailing of the two-year-old turned hysterical, and he was taken into his mother's arms and cradled there even as the woman continued to direct the other children in their tasks. The woman bounced the toddler gently on her left knee; she dug and pointed with one hand, caressed with the other. The child's crying continued, but slowly lost its urgency. The other children were busily at work, digging and patting. The mother continued to rock the boy gently in her lap until suddenly he was silent. Faye noticed that in a split second the boy had fallen asleep. In that moment of silence something shifted in her. She didn't understand it, but she wondered then if perhaps perfection was something to be found outside of herself. (Napoleon tossed in his sleep.) Surely silence is what we are born from. She tapped Michael on the arm.

"I'm hungry," she said adamantly.

They packed up and went to an expensive restaurant. Faye's sleep was restless that night, and the next morning they caught a plane to Rome.

Her arm is stiff from propping up her head. She closes the fashion magazine, gets up from the floor, and goes into their bedroom. The clothes she wore to the funeral are scattered on a chair. She hangs them up and takes out other clothes—summer dresses she hasn't worn in years. She tries two or three, slipping into them effortlessly, but the shapes are different and she feels clumsy inside them. The brassiere seams of the long black rayon dress with halter straps fall higher than they should. She cups her breasts, pushing them up. Better. With two fingers, she pins up the sides of her face in a surgical lift. *Tuck tuck.* Better. She was so young on Elba.

Back in Toronto she resumed her place as third cello in the orchestra, but the din of dissatisfaction remained. She attempted to quiet it by experimenting with new work. She ventured outside the orchestra's repertoire into contemporary music: Stockhausen, Boulez, Shaffer—open-ended, unresolved sounds that suited her well. When Michael came home she'd cover up the scores and breathlessly run through descending chords in Haydn.

She tidied a lot. Picking up papers and cups in the living room where Michael sat reading the newspaper, she tried to get his attention.

"What would you think about a French name for a child?" she said, testing the waters.

Michael didn't look up, but cleared his throat before he answered.

"French names are nice."

Encouraged, she pushed a little farther. "You mean, you think we should give our child a French name?"

He looked at her. "What do you mean?"

"I mean, if we had one, of course," she said, backing off slightly.

"I don't see why not." He went back to his paper.

She couldn't tell if Michael was open to the idea or not. "Would you want one?"

"When the time comes," he said calmly.

She continued to tidy, and took to polishing the wood and silver as though they were part of a new instrument, humming the new pieces she'd been practising in secret. Very slowly, an obsession coalesced around the perfect doll-like bodies of two- and three-year-old children she would see with their mothers in the street. She would smile at them, being often ignored, but on occasion feeling a strong connection. At the bookstore she fingered pages of books about procreation, researching the whole gamut—from the copulation of the most basic organisms in the animal kingdom to the complex mating habits and reproduction of humans. On slow afternoons she'd pull Dr. Spock from the shelf and read snippets behind the counter. All through the fall of that year she dreamt about tiny hands, transparent fingernails. When she woke in the middle of the night from these intense dreams she would touch her body to see if it had been transformed, to see if Michael had changed her, but no, there she was, the same. She would watch him sleeping and wonder how consciousness could be so lost, how a distance so deep into sleep could ever be reversed and if he would ever wake up. Sleep chose him, abandoning her to staring, staring, staring, while long lines of fatigue grew near her nose.

One morning near Christmas, she threw away her pills in a gesture that felt sufficiently reckless to nudge her out of inertia. She didn't tell Michael. He continued to wake her up in the morning by rolling over to hug her and press his erection up against her back.

After two months of secretly hoping she was pregnant and alternately dreading that she might be, she began to keep track of her reproductive cycle. She counted the days, one to fourteen, then ovulation, the *slip, plop* of a delicate egg. She made sure that on her ripe-egg morning she was especially affectionate. Michael responded with new interest. It was so unexpected she became suspicious. Did he know what she was up to? Was he calling her bluff? They reversed rolls in bed; she became the distant one, thinking only of the end and not enjoying the means.

Still nothing. She was conscious of her breasts swelling, each time hoping they were fat pregnant breasts and not the sign of a bloated period. The cycles of notes and eggs continued for almost a year. Michael's work progressed well, the orchestra was offered a tour of Western Canada and received a grant for a commissioned piece. Faye's playing plateaued, even regressed some days so that she couldn't play some of the simplest pieces. Finding it hard to concentrate, she asked for more hours at the bookstore, where she read curious accounts of mating, such as how snails strive for fatherhood by throwing darts at their mates. The mucous-coated love darts penetrate the partner's skin during mating and carry substances that boost the sperm's chance of fertilising eggs. Similarly, the corkscrew shape of the pig penis and the thick mucous seal after ejaculation help to ensure that pig sperm and pig egg get trapped together and have no option but to join.

One day, after riding home on a bumpy streetcar where a foul-smelling man had thrown up over her shoes, it became all too much. *Fuck, fuck, fuck.*

"Puke couldn't find a better target," she said, bursting simultaneously into tears and Michael's studio: "I'm useless, nothing comes, nothing, not even the most common thing in nature . . ." and then she was out of breath. Michael looked confounded.

"Sit down, you're upset," he ventured. She began to wail. He didn't know what to do. He got up to guide her to his armchair. "Calm down. What are you talking about?" She sniffed and choked on tears that were filling up every opening in her head. He rubbed her shoulders. "That's it, now take deep breaths. Relax. You're good, gifted, lovely . . . a spring of life," he said.

His words had sprung from the third movement of Mahler's 4th Symphony he had been studying. They annoyed her. To hurt him, she told him what she'd been doing with her body—their bodies.

"How could—" he sputtered, and his hand fell from her shoulder. He walked out of the room and slammed the door behind him. His anger sent her further into despair, she wailed until he came in again.

"Faye . . . listen to me . . . I love you . . . you could have told me."

"We'll die otherwise," she gasped through her sobs, not really knowing what she meant.

"You're young," he said, "we have plenty of time."

"But do you want one?" She saw him hesitate.

"If you want to try, that's what we'll do."

She vanished inside him again.

She began to chart the rise and fall of her temperature around ovulation, waking up early with the sun, and the peep of the digital thermometer would wake Michael. After intercourse she'd lie for half an hour coaching the sperm along, visualising them reaching the egg, penetrating the membrane. For the following two weeks she'd walk around their apartment rubbing her tummy and playing silly expectant-parent games.

"How about Genevieve?"

"Mmm, that's nice," Michael would say from behind a score.

"But Genevieve Ryan doesn't work; neither does Genevieve Seaton. No, let's try something else."

It would go like that through the Brigittes, Giselles, Manons, and Dominiques, until they settled on an Irish name, from her grandfather: Sean, for a girl or a boy. Sean Ryan Seaton.

But in no time she was thirty and still had not missed a period. She decided it was time to see a specialist, and was referred to a clinic in Hamilton by her gynaecologist. She would be in good hands there; doctors at the clinic were at the forefront of research into infertility.

Infertility. It had been named and she became the word the way Sean would have become the sibilant flow of those four letters had the child been born. They underwent tests: First a laparoscopy on Faye to check for scar tissue, for endometrial scattering. They found none. Then on Michael, a semen analysis. The results suggested that he avoid hot baths, wear boxer shorts, and take large doses of vitamins B and C. A few weeks later he was tested again and all was adequate, perfect. After intercourse, Faye had to rush to the gynaecologist for a test to see whether sperm and host mucous were compatible.

Ya suck out the centre of a raw egg and lie on ya back . . . Faye recalls the tone of certainty in Simon's mother's voice as she described the obeah method of slapped belly and spins. Is it possible that Faye and Michael had overlooked something elemental—all those mornings with her coaching sperm and egg to join? Still, months later, nothing. Lying on the bed now, she lifts her legs up into the air.

Back at the fertility clinic she had a hysterosalpinogram, which examined whether or not her tubes and uterus could transport and sustain a fertilised egg. Doctors injected them with a dye that could be traced passing through or being blocked, the way water in a drain might clog or flow. The pain was excruciating, as plumbing might have been, but she was clean.

On Michael they performed a varicocele, checking for veins around the testicles that might raise its temperature thereby lowering the sperm count. A stethoscope was attached to his testicles and the sound amplified in stereo. At first Michael found the concept amusing, but the second test, in which his sperm was placed in a dish with a hamster egg to see if it was capable of penetrating it, was humiliating. He was visibly offended and became moody and distant. All tests came back negative; there was nothing technically wrong with them. They had idiopathic infertility. Her joke became that she was the idiot and he was the path . . . *ha, ha,* but then her spirits sank. Michael became defiant. Befitting his character, he wouldn't succumb to someone else's assessment of his abilities or nature. Don Giovanni in D-minor: *"No! No! No! No!"* He tried even harder, and every morning, no matter where she was in her cycle, he tapped her on the back with a throb, rolled her over, and made ferocious love.

It worked.

In 1785, when Leopold Mozart received a letter from Joseph Haydn that stated "Before God and as an honest man I tell you that your son is the greatest composer known to me either in person or by name," the great one's sister was expecting her first child. Resentment . . . rancour . . . ridiculous . . . ruin, ruin, ruin. Was the sound of *r* in Nannerl's guts when she first vomited into her chamber pot on a cold December morning? Could she taste *r* in the traces of bile that followed her food into the pot? Was there any music to accompany it?

Although pleased to have thrown the dirty word infertility back in the faces of the specialists, when Faye realised she was really pregnant, when the period—so aptly named for ending expectations as well as sentences—didn't arrive, she was vile with panic. Suddenly she wanted to play again, loudly, ferociously, tearing the strings with her bow. She didn't want to be pregnant, didn't want to be dictated by her body. But she had no choice; she had willed it, had colluded with Michael against herself and had to bear the consequences. And Nannerl, Faye's unrehearsed self, visited her like the ghostly guest of an unwritten opera.

By the third month she had resigned herself to the nausea

and even relished the idea of fat. For the first time in her life she could feel more than just bone along her hips. She wanted more. Some days there was fear, other days excitement and giddiness. Michael spoiled her with special meals and gifts, extra attention so uncharacteristic that she would grow irritable, still not understanding her own dissatisfaction. She attributed any dissonance to the hormonal changes taking place inside her. She was the world, creating itself, exploding.

At the end of her third month, Faye finally decided to let her parents know about the pregnancy. Without telling Michael, she visited them unannounced, arriving feeling smug and fat. After greeting Faye, her mother retreated into the orange armchair, the same one she would eventually die in. She had coloured her hair brown, and her face was caked in powder, as though she'd applied it in the dark. Faye's stomach did a slow backward somersault. She looked into her mother's eyes, hoping to see an opening for a discussion about pregnancy, labour, the swoosh of emotion she was feeling, but the eyes locked her out. *Slam, slam* . . . the sound of doors everywhere. Michael . . . *slam* . . . Mother . . . *slam*. Faye shuddered. She stayed for only a short while, asking her mother polite questions about her health . . . *dry the dishes, dry the dishes* . . . and about her father who was at the track, loving his horses, his wild Irish horses, not this plucked swan sitting staring out the window.

Faye couldn't go home. She decided to go down to the lake. Harbourfront, in late autumn, would not be too busy, and she could find herself a quiet spot and stare out at the islands. The wind was strong, the smell of the lake was harsh and fishy, and she strolled along the quay to work off the chill. On either side of the docks a few boats sat in their winter berths. A group of teenage boys stood on the bridge arcing over the docks, smoking, talking in code, laughing. They had cartoon haircuts, their heads shaved and spiked like the backs of ailing porcupines. One of them spit regularly, hurling his saliva as far as he could in the face of the wind. *Oh where oh where has my little dog gone* . . . Faye began to hum, over and over as she came from beneath the bridge. *With his tail cut short and his ears cut long, oh where* . . . *Whack!* Something hit her on the back of her head; a ball of spit smeared into her hair. *Whoop Whoop!* The boys swayed with laughter. Her blood boiled. She wanted to tear at them, to rip out their gobby tongues. She didn't want her body invaded by something that could ever become like them.

She walked home quickly, leaning into gusts of wind bearing down from the northwest. When she got home, she exploded into Michael's studio, telling him what a mess it was, how the whole house was a mess, *filth, filth, filth* . . . *ya filthy beast, can't you even clean up after yourself?* Michael stared, unblinking, stunned. Faye slammed more doors and locked herself in her studio, not practising, just sitting, staring too. All of them staring.

Lying on the bed tonight, her legs still raised above her, Faye is embarrassed to remember herself in such a swampy state of emotions.

Two weeks later, her mother died. Into the fourth month of her pregnancy, Faye miscarried.

One month, two, then three, feeling sorry . . . *oh me, oh my* . . . for herself, but she slowly regained her determination. Her friend Mary suggested she give sniffing musk a try as a way to increase her fertility. Animal musk is similar in composition to testosterone; experiments conducted by a new perfume company had revealed that women who sniffed musk developed shorter menstrual cycles, ovulated more often, and found it easier to conceive. Faye had snorted with laughter at the idea. She didn't tell Michael about Mary's suggestion and the next day made another appointment at the fertility clinic.

A new doctor offered her a part in an *in vitro* fertilisation trial. The procedure was then experimental, usually used only for proven tubal blockage or immobile sperm. She would be part of a study. She consented. The dice rolled. She had always been terrified of injections, but quickly had to overcome any uneasiness. "Shooting up," she began to call it. "Let's shoot," she'd moan to Michael, after readying the syringe full of Pergonal and Metrodin. The mixture would provoke ovulation, and then she'd trek to the hospital to test her oestrogen levels to prevent an explosion of eggs. At first Faye made fun of the procedure, calling out "Action!" as Michael wiped her buttocks with alcohol before piercing her with the syringe, but soon, as her buttocks turned black and blue and the torment of blood tests, cervix prodding, and ultrasound piled up, she grew fragile. Pergonal was purgatory. She swung between morose and comatose and cried non-stop.

She stopped playing in the orchestra, other than as a stand-in, by mutual agreement. Some days even working at the bookstore was too much. By the time they finally removed six of her ova, introduced Michael's sperm to each in separate petri dishes, and then reimplanted the tiny embryo, she had lost all sense of who she was. She was a monster, a raving, hungering beast who sucked up the very notion of eggs, of embryos, of fetuses, of babies. She'd imagine the laboratory filled with the eggs of equally desperate participants and at night dream that doctors had implanted embryos from the wrong dish, that some other couple's gametes were trying to survive in her uterus. And the eggs they'd frozen, what happened to them? Who owned them now? What kind of place was this?

The first implantation didn't take; the second took but failed just a few days later. Then another, but *slip, slip*, off it slid from her uterine wall. Thousands of dollars later and with her hormones wired for detonation, Michael convinced Faye that they should stop, at least for a while.

Michael suffered his own setbacks. Negotiations for a recording contract for the orchestra fell through and he was demoralised. His interest in teaching diminished and his conducting grew lacklustre, but Faye was unable to provide comfort, unable to enter his failure—her role for him had not allowed for that. One day, as he stood with his back turned to her, she found herself singing out: "*Anima di bronzo*" as Leporello to his master Don Giovanni. Where had that come from? Surely this was not true, not a soul of iron, not this man who had given her the subtle gifts of his heart and mind. She was frightened by thoughts that began to possess her. She sought out other passages from the opera, seeking again the erotic pitch of Donna Anna, and found a sudden C-minor chord ... *brass, that's it, now the stringendo of the strings rising in thirds* ... and tried to hold on to the moment, just as Donna Anna holds on to the sleeve of her seducer so firmly that he is unable to tear himself loose.

Faye's legs are numb from being raised too long in the air. She lies flat and welcomes the next memory as a relative ... *hello self* ... something else she can draw from tonight.

Although she had begun to feel that she couldn't have a child because she was still one herself, she went back on Pergonal. Sleeplessness and Pergonal. This time it was worse. Hallucinations. She would hear paper bags coming to life, watch lamps dancing in the living room, feel chairs exhale as she sat on them. While sipping tea with Mary in a cafe, she felt her body expand, grow out of the chair, out of her clothes. Believing everyone was witnessing her flesh bursting out of her shirt, Faye excused herself. She felt like Alice, unable to be contained by the space around her which was insufficiently feeding her desires. "*Goodbye feet! ... oh my poor little feet, I wonder who will put on your shoes and stockings for you now, dears ... how queer everything is today ... who in the world am I?*"

By the time she felt herself returning to normal, she had run to her car, clutching her clothes about her. Too embarrassed to return to Mary, she decided to go home, but realised she was now ravenous. She stopped at a grocery store to buy something

to eat. In an aisle with cereal, she spotted a little boy, just three
or four years old, standing alone, lost in thought, staring at the
colourful boxes on the shelves. Faye looked around. No one.
Only a few questions crossed her mind, none of which was
whether she had the right to intervene. She pulled the child up
by the arm and walked quickly with him, out the automatic
door and into the parking lot. She heard only one thing—not
his cries of protest, not anyone asking questions—only her own
ballooning cells. She felt she had to work fast before she got too
big and was unable to fit into the car to drive away. She barely
thought of the boy, except with some certainty that she was
acting out of mutual necessity. Before she was able to put the
key in the lock, she was accosted by security guards, bystanders,
and the wailing mother.

Only now can she imagine the scene. Then, it was all white
noise, a distraction from the sound of her expanding protoplasm.
She was admitted to hospital and stayed for several weeks,
deprived of sharp objects, pumped with pills to induce calm:
Noritriptyline, Desipramine, Amitriptyline. She sang them, over
and over, pronouncing their common ending like the German
ein and sang a little night music before she drowsed off, which
was often. In the mornings she was woken by a psychiatrist
whom she had to convince that it had been the Pergonal that
had caused her behaviour. *Wash the dishes, dry the dishes* . . . .

Finally, she was released. At home, she avoided Michael,
avoided music, read more but left the bookstore and looked for
other work. She watched Michael sleep night after night, as the
distance between them grew. Two things belong to everyone:
love and sleep. But sleep was a vacuum draining her. And love
was impenetrable. In a few weeks she moved out.

It felt painful, cruel, and her guilt was enormous. She stayed
with Mary for awhile, then started a telemarketing job and got
her own apartment. She saw Michael a few times, showing up
at his house like a stray, always on the verge of running back to

him. But she'd stay only a short while; he'd pour her a cup of coffee and ask how she was, and then the memory of the shrinking and growing would become too strong and she'd leave again. The urge to go back to him eventually died away, but she continued to be propelled by the force of what had drawn her to him, the sheer drive of notes and tempo—the unvanquished demon inside her. When she met Simon, she was grateful for his silence.

She gets up from the bed and walks back to her studio, picks up her cello and tunes it, stretching her fingers down its neck. She plays quickly, furiously, bending Bach, her bow flying over the strings, her left hand diving up the neck to the split-string harmonics. She must come out of the past. Music awakens it, and with it comes tingling—and much pain—as the body throws off numbness. After she left Michael she couldn't play. She felt like an adolescent in the blue aftermath of love. Her days were blemished and awkward, but she busied herself, trying to numb parts of her consciousness. Leaving Michael was like leaving part of herself, a trapped coyote chewing off its own leg. Guilt, loss, and a limping future. She tried to think of herself as an organism unto itself, alone and self-regenerating. A worm. This worked for some time, until she met Simon and felt the need leak out again. She tugs her bow; rosin smokes the air . . .

During the mating ritual, the male octopus alternates stroking the female with each of his eight arms. The third arm feels for the genital opening, while caressing continues with the other seven. Discovering that opening, still caressing as distraction, it pumps packets of sperm into her.

A pinch of eighth notes . . . her fingers fly . . .

Blue fish in the Pacific are bisexual.

. . . high C . . .

Female elephants are sexually receptive for only a few days every four years or so.

. . . andante . . .

Barnacles have the longest sexual organ possessed by any animal, and each has a male and female component. Barnacles are efficient, mating without much effort, from either end, at any time, with any other. Anima/animus animals.

A last violent arpeggio . . . Her fingers trot along the cello's neck. She attacks the strings with her bow; it flies from her hand, hitting the mirror. *Wuwhhaack!*

The sound rings through the house. She cups a hand over her gasp and listens. Did he hear it? There is movement in the living room, as he shuffles about.

Is he looking for something . . . did he see me hide the envelope? I hear the tinkling of glass and ice. Has he remembered the bottle of rum he brought home yesterday?

I'm afraid to go down. I reach down through the floor, across the ceiling, my pointed fingertip reaching, reaching . . . just to touch . . . oh . . .

He's returning to the basement.

CHAPTER 5

Salt

Slouched in his chair, shivers chiming along his skin, Simon slips his hand into his pocket to feel for the compass. The brass case is warmer than his fingers. He runs his thumb along its circumference, fondles the latch, then grips the warm disc in his palm. He doesn't remove it from the pocket, not yet; he's not ready. The report on the Scarborough Bluffs lies open at the first page on his desk.

He tries to concentrate on the project of sand, reaching back to his studies, but feels encumbered by the years of cross-referencing that have dulled his skills. He's increasingly uncomfortable with the distance he's travelled from the science that originally inspired him, and is secretly relieved about the prospect of losing his job. But last week the director of the cartography division hinted that in the restructuring Simon could be offered one of the sought-after management positions in the Ministry of Transport when the reorganisation is complete. Simon is haunted by a future of piles: memos, progress reports, and complaints that would settle on him like sediment.

"Ya have to be practical," Edwin had said to him one evening after inviting him into the library for a chat. "Choose something that lasts, something that people will always need. Things change, jobs become obsolete, then there you are, unable to feed yourself, much less your family." His family? Had he ever given enough thought to that?

In bed one afternoon after they first met, as her fingers lingered along his chest, Faye told Simon about the fertility clinic. Making light of her trials there, she joked that she and Michael could have found ways of limiting the height of their

child using gene therapy if they had wanted a medium-sized
child. Isolating the gene for height and manipulating it in a
zygote before implantation into the uterus could give them the
desired height. "But the bigger the better these days." She smiled
and curled her long leg over his. Michael and Faye would have
had a very tall child—like the many Simon has seen here in
Canada—a two-year-old who looks five. Small line-backers with
big necks and heads, speaking the same English of two-year-
olds heard around the world, but theirs with bigger tones, extra
weight behind "no" and "want." He remembers Faye telling
him that each time they implanted her with multiple embryos,
she would dream of iguanas crawling out of her and puffing out
accusing chins. Making love to her afterwards, all Simon could
see was iguana faces morphing into the face of a child they
might be making. His flat nose, her tiny head, his skin, her eyes,
their hands—all in the 3:1 ratio of possible occurrence he'd
learned about in his first year of university.

At Harrison College, Simon received first-class honours in
his A level chemistry, biology, physics, geography, and maths and
was expecting to be accepted at all three of the universities to
which he had applied. When his father had asked him what he
wanted, Simon had to suppress the word that had crystallised on
his tongue over many years: salt. Instead, he mumbled something about being useful and understanding the composition of
the world. Out flew Edwin's speech about practicality, and
Simon pictured David's grin—a grin that flew in the face of the
silences that Simon had once tried to wield.

"What about engineering?" Edwin suggested. The word
carved the first angles of the container Simon would occupy
much of his life. Even by the time his family was assembled to
see him off, his decision made little sense. He was enrolled at
Queen's University in Kingston, Canada; geological engineering
was a speciality at Queen's. Almost two years to the day after

they had bid goodbye to David, Simon sweltered through his own leave-taking at Grantly Adams Airport. His suit was not hand-made by his mother, but had been specially purchased for his journey north, along with fashionable platform shoes that gave him desired height.

His father rushed about checking details over and over, making sure Simon's papers were in order, asking the attendants at the departure gate about seating, arrival times, and expected flying conditions. Edwin's nervousness revealed his pride—a blushing body propelled him around the open space of the terminal. So different from his taciturnity and the allusions to sinking at David's departure, which had weighed down on the whole family.

As the time approached for boarding, Simon moved closer to Edith, who stood dutifully by to bid him farewell. He wanted to press his groin to hers one last time, but with his family watching all he could manage was to brush her hip. He dabbed her bottom lip with his baby finger and it swelled beneath his skin. "Sly mongoose . . ." he whispered in her ear.

He kissed Maggie, letting her whisper-chide him for dismantling his aquarium of coral and tiger fish and not giving it to her. Her eyes were hidden by her waterfall curls. He wondered if she was indifferent to his departure. But he caught a glimpse of glassy green light behind a ringlet and could see that her eyes were teary. He gulped and took a deep breath.

Francie embraced Simon and said, "You promise to come back, 'cause I don't think I could bear it without either of my brothers." She released him and looked straight into his eyes: "And remember: BWIA . . ." Simon caught her growing smile and knew his cue. In unison they recited: "Britain's Worst Investment Abroad! Better Walk If Able!" and both giggled, Francie choking back tears. Phillip rubbed Francie's back. Simon could sense something between them. His brotherly protectiveness rose, as he was all too aware of Phillip's romantic reputation. And since the decision to grow dreadlocks and reclaim his roots, Phillip's passion for roots music, roots food, roots pleasure, and roots love had become a source of anxiety for his best friend. But in a flash, Phillip was performing again, and the sorcery of his mime overtook Simon's fears.

Phillip pulled Simon aside. One hand, hidden under his T-shirt, pumped like a harrowed heart trying to break free. His face gathered into ridges, the skin creased like a beast's in sorrow, and Simon could have sworn Phillip had aged twenty years right before him. Then tears trickled down the creased flesh and Phillip whispered in a delicate nibble at Simon's ear: "Dragons cry ..."

Simon closed his eyes to hold back a sob, and when he opened them Phillip was gone. He didn't understand the performance. Perhaps there was something he'd overlooked in the sign he shared with his father. Dragons were ferocious, feared, slain by knights—reptilian birds that spit fire. Unconquerable beasts. For years after, the mime would tease him, but he could never interpret it. He considered what Phillip had told him about crocodiles, which are said to shed tears at the moment they bite into their prey—was this also true of dragons? Among the twelve Chinese astrological signs—dogs, rats, pigs, roosters, and so on—the dragon stood out. Dragons were not real. They came from nowhere, belonged nowhere.

Simon gave each of his family a last, distracted kiss. MacKenzie loosened his tie and, with her handkerchief, wiped sweat from his brow and from around his neck. She was humming a vaguely familiar tune. The words came to him slowly: *When you walk through a storm, hold your head up high ...* His mother straightened his lapels, patted his shoulders, and then stood back to examine him. She backed up—*or was it me?*—waved goodbye, then raised her right foot to her left calf before blowing a kiss. Simon backed through the security gate.

When the sliding glass doors closed, all he could see was his own reflection.

As the plane climbed into the air, he opened his eyes and raised his hand to wave goodbye, but the aircraft had moved well beyond the airport. He looked down at the sea shattering into white surf along the rocks of the east coast and spotted the lighthouse at Ragged Point. He pressed his forehead against the window. Flashes of black torpedoes breaking the blue sea, splashing white. Had he seen right? A flock—the same flock of pelicans? He grew dizzy, and a bell ringing above him was followed by the captain's voice announcing that it was safe to unbuckle seat belts.

Simon is cold again. The house is silent. Of what does trust consist? Of the earth? Or of the sky that limits it? *It's almost eleven o'clock; she must be asleep. I can't hear her.*

They had talked through the night, even as Mary slept on the chair beside them. The other couples in David's apartment had started to stir again—bodies buzzing beyond the thin walls—when Simon and Faye fell silent. Simon looked at his hands.

"You like games," he said with certainty.

"I guess so," Faye offered, sleepily now.

"Turn your back to me."

She did as he asked. Through the kitchen window she saw the glow of the sun inch higher. The magic of the scorpion evening was receding; Faye began to feel self-conscious. She heard him move, then felt his hand on her back. She closed her eyes. He ran a finger across her cotton camisole, touching one bare shoulder, then the other. His touch stopped and continued again in a circle the other way. She felt the outline of the thing he had stitched to her. He paused.

"So, what is it?" he asked finally.

"A wing," she said, stupidly.

"No, try again."

He repeated the pattern, but still she couldn't guess.

"It's salt, a crystal, magnified a million times, now worked into your skin . . . you're safe."

"Safe?"

"When salt works on flesh it doesn't allow corruption, it carries off bad odours, drives off filth, worms . . . destroys impurities."

"But—"

"That's what MacKenzie, our maid back home, told me all my life, but I mean it biochemically, whereas she talks about God, about blessing penetrating and exorcising . . . 'souls not salted with Christ's words begin to smell' . . ."

Faye turned around. His face looked harder than it had earlier in the night. She reached up and brushed it with her fingers. He didn't look at her, but took her hand and held it to his cheek, unconsciously rubbing her hand with his fingers, back and forth, as though trying to warm it. Their palms, both meshed with the same code of lines, as though they'd once been attached, met. A part of her—deeper than Michael, as deep as the idea of Sean or the music of Mozart—stirred. It stretched with a gasping, wakening yawn. He placed her hand back at her side. The deepness rolled over and nodded off again.

"MacKenzie used to tease me that the ice in Canada would make me thirsty. I never used to listen to her. I always thought what she said was full of country superstition . . . ignorance."

Faye reached down beside the chair that propped up her sleeping friend and picked up her purse. Simon's drowsy eyes followed without registering her movement.

"Did you know that seventy-five percent of all the world's fresh water is stored in glaciers?"

Faye took a pen and paper out of her bag and wrote down

her name and phone number. She was struggling not to fall under a spell. Her limbs felt slack, as if the muscles had turned into strings waiting to be pulled. Simon watched her leave the number on the kitchen table. Faye didn't bother to wake Mary. She left quickly.

Coral and shells. Barbados is a coral bed risen from the sea, an island of pressed shoal. When Simon arrived in Kingston and saw the limestone ridges, the similarity was comforting. He'd travelled by bus from Toronto, along the road carved through the granite of the Canadian Shield that marked the left-hand side of the highway like a shoreline. The lake glistened to the right. The scenery was a mosaic of granite rock and gold- and red-turning leaves. Rock had been blasted out to allow asphalt. What audacity, he thought, that a man could believe he should blast the earth for his purposes—a billion years of rock, gone with a stick of dynamite, for a path somewhere.

Kingston was vined. Buildings made of white stone that had once been the bottom of a sea were shingled with ivy. It was a city struggling to surface and it suited Simon immediately.

On the first day of the week-long initiation ceremonies at Queen's, Simon was given a torn piece of tartan, a jumbo safety pin, and a tam, and was told to report to the stairs of Miller Hall. Well-built young men with the tell-tale posture and mannerisms of wealth stretched out over the stairs and entrance, some of them already wearing torn kilts over their bare bottoms. Leaders were organising lines of freshman and forcing them to drink a purple concoction—"purple Jesus"—yelling abuses . . . *dumb Frosh* . . . and shoving them into line to dance a can-can while singing a song Simon couldn't quite make out: *Oil thigh nebrandigan . . . nebrandigan . . . something something . . .* *"Louder! Louder dumb Frosh!"*

Simon thought of Guyana, of the demonstration in Stabroek market: *I'm the king of the castle . . .*

Someone grabbed him, snatched the tam out of his hands, and shoved it onto his head, flattening his curls. He was dragged over to a large metal tub filled with purple dye.

. . . and you're the dirty rascal.

Some frosh were being thrown into the tub; others were wiped with the dye that wine-stained them head to foot. It was his turn. The leader of the Frosh group took Simon's arm and started to paint his shoulder with a purple-stained cloth. He painted and painted. Nothing was happening. The dye wasn't taking. The leader soaked the cloth again and squeezed the violet water onto Simon's leg. Just a darker brown, no purple. He stopped, flung the cloth aside, speechless, while a flush, like inner ink, travelled from his thick neck slowly towards his ears. He stammered something about the arm being green, kicked at the bucket, and moved on callously to the next quivering victim. Simon picked up his things and walked calmly back to his room, remaining there for the next six days, only leaving for meals in the cafeteria just before it closed.

Classes started the next week. His studies went well. Chemistry, physics, mineralogy, mathematics, and two electives: biology, and a course in philosophy "to keep MacKenzie happy and God at bay," as his father had advised him before leaving. The moral clarity of science possessed him in those early weeks. He revelled in the hypothetical, the discovery of balance and symmetry. He thought most about his father in biology class, wondering how he had survived the indignities of veterinary college in the 1950s at the University of Guelph, his Guyana bush and river logic beside the blonde reason of Canada.

Gregor Mendel was a monk working in the Augustinian monastery of St. Thomas in Moravia. Using the garden pea to examine inherited characteristics, his experiments were simple and founded on the best principles of science: well-selected species, a few selected traits, a limited experiment that could be extrapolated to the larger world. Round-seeded peas were crossed with wrinkled-seeded peas by removing the anthers of the one, so they could not self-pollinate, and then brushing the stigmas with the pollen from the other. In the second generation some peas were round, some wrinkled, according to a 3:1 ratio. Inheritance could follow simple arithmetical rules. The patterns were not invariably messy, not the mixing of inks. The peas were either wrinkled or they were not—not half-wrinkled or wrinkled in parts. The quality of wrinkledness had not been diluted, and still less had it been extinguished. It merely had been suppressed for a generation. Simon expanded this pattern to multiple characteristics, to bits and pieces of heredity, and his family fell into place. Maggie's blonde hair, green eyes; David's African brow; Francie's Indian pout; his own Semitic curls. When he read about the identification of DNA in 1868 by the Swiss scientist who coded the chemistry of the nucleus, he felt that the code was simply too beautiful not to be true. His life lifted off high above Garden Gap in Christ Church, Barbados.

Soon his enchantment expanded beyond biology class and took shape in crystals—the salt crystals he examined under the microscope and the ice crystals of snow, which he experienced for the first time. The dreamy first snowfall found him trudging through a sleepy world, marvelling at the disguises snow offered nature, neutralising buildings and roads. He wrote a long letter home describing the patterns and textures. At Christmas, alone but for two other foreign students in the dorm, he telephoned his family and tried to describe the way the snow glittered and reflected the festive lights. Trying to get all her news in before Maggie grabbed the receiver, Francie told him, almost in one breath, that she had just taken a job in a fashion boutique at a hotel and that he should lie down in the snow and make angels the way they did in the movies. Simon laughed and said he would. But as the winter wore on, the snow became more and more frightening; another snowfall would surely destroy the trees, another patch of ice would mean his extinction, or at least his mutation as he adapted to its aggression. Snow had a power the ocean was not capable of. A quilt of death covered the streets, deceivingly protective ... *approaching again, outside, coming in the wind.*

The cold was useful; he was never tempted to diversion as he had been in Barbados. Cricket was out of the question; winter sports unimaginable. He had nothing else to do but study in his small single room in Morris Hall—the only co-ed dorm on campus—while cashmere sweaters sprouted like hairy mushrooms on the chests of the young women around him. None of them seemed to mind the winter; they were capable, strong girls whom Francie and her friends would have called "he–shes," ridiculing them for undecorated faces and plain hair. But the understatement gave their mushrooming bosoms even more mysterious power over Simon. The cold deterred him from pursuing sex, but at night, aroused, he had dreams of breasts that he swayed over and eventually sprayed, a careful watering so they'd grow more and more. The cashmere was moss he fertilised each night.

During the day, he thought of Edith's full, ribbed lips on his ears. Picturing them during class he would get aroused. He wanted to hear her cry "shit, shit, oh shit" and to be gripped by the tiny convulsions between her legs.

"You want to visit?" he asked her on the phone one Sunday. Edith's father had money and could afford to send her, whereas Simon couldn't afford passage home for two years. In late May he would begin work picking asparagus on a farm north of Kingston instead of liming on the beach with Phillip. He had a free week after exams and would be allowed to keep his dorm room until his job started.

Edith booked her flight.

"Stop that ... people're lookin," she complained at the train station when he held her close and kissed her. He looked around but there was no one in sight. Edith frowned in the taxi, frowned when she saw the two-storey residence, and when he opened the door to his small single room she gasped an "Oh God," that spat at his remaining lust. He watched her unpack with growing panic and nausea, wondering why he'd never noticed how little he had to say to her, and searching for the secret in her that had eclipsed her ugly face. He longed for the perverse pleasure of the previous summer, the peeling back of his skin by her lips, his fingers anointed with her trust. Had it been a trick?

He tried to touch her again, to return to the murmur of assurance he had heard inside her, a sound he had sought throughout his life.

"You crushin' my dress, Simon. Behave."

He fraudulently patted his pillows and pulled the bedspread down, feeling like a rake.

"You hungry? I'm starvin'," he said to escape his regret. "Why don't we go out for dinner?"

When they returned from a diner in the student ghetto, they passed three female nursing students, whose exams were still in progress, along the hall. Beers in hand, and discussing bone fractures, they made way for Simon and Edith to pass and, almost in unison, uttered a polite, "Hi, Simon," then disappeared into the lounge.

"Friendly fa so," Edith said under her breath. Simon hadn't the courage to tell her that the greeting represented most of his interactions with the girls in the dorm, but Edith took his silence as a switch in allegiance.

"Well, well," she sang sarcastically, and his jaw clenched. He fought back the urge to beg her to understand how much he wanted the blue and the buzzing and the fragrance and the salt, but that this was all he had now, what he was meant to do. He wanted to go home.

The next day they walked the streets of Kingston, Simon trying to impart to her his new knowledge of Canadian history, but forcing her to walk unspeakable distances for a Bajan. When they returned to the dorm she was exhausted. They saw one of the nursing students again, who gave them a friendly smile.

"These people think we're not worth a hello or a chat or a come around for a drink?"

"It's not like at home, people are trying to get somewhere," Simon defended; he couldn't bring himself to agree with her and wonder together why he had spent the last eight months mostly alone.

He loathed himself for his treachery, and for his vanity, thinking that the cashmere mushroom girls might have noticed Edith's ugliness. In bed that night, she finally let him touch her, but remained silent while he made furious love to her, shaking the tiny cheap bed until it rattled loose. He carved her like the sea carves stone, making a cave, a place to hide.

They spent the next week sitting down by the lake—a shabby, cold substitute for the sea, according to Edith—and then making love in his room. In the evening he would sneak food for her from the cafeteria, which they ate sitting on the broken bed with their backs propped against the wall. They slept a lot, talked very little; he asked her about home and for gossip; she offered little except her punctuating observations of Kingston life. He found himself defending Canada and northern girls for their schooling.

"I'd never live in such a horrible cold country with cold people," she pronounced finally. When she left he was so relieved he threw himself into the lake, trying to cleanse his guilt and to baptise this new man he'd become: sullied, dangerous, and as severed from the dreaming beach-cricket boy in Garden

Gap as a coral necklace is from a reef. The lake water was icy, the absence of salt a shock, and he sank heavily. He never answered Edith's many letters after that trip.

When he ran into her in Bridgetown the summer after his third year at Queen's, it was the first contact with her since the visit to Kingston. Her face had changed, softened. She greeted him exuberantly, seeming oblivious to his discomfiture. She told him about her correspondence with a Canadian man she'd met while he was on holiday in Barbados, and how he'd sent her passage to Toronto the previous summer. He'd taken her to the Canadian National Exhibition where she'd ridden the roller coaster and the spinning polar ride. They'd dined at an expensive restaurant at the top of one of the tallest buildings in the city, and from there she had gazed out over the world. He sent her things bought at the Hudson's Bay Company, Eaton's— clothes, dinnerware for her mother, books with photographs of loons, lakes, and the wilderness of the Canadian Shield. Proudly showing off the label of her Holt Renfrew shirt, she said "It's expensive, but quality is quality," and Simon's spirits sank. What must it have meant to her to show him that label? He imagined Edith on a ferris wheel circling her own fears, over and over, and understood how far into herself she'd had to travel to confront what she'd hated in him. It was the first time Simon glimpsed the mechanism of loss: how becoming like the thing you miss is a way of leaving it behind.

When she parted from him with a cheerful, "Great to see you," he suddenly missed Canada. But Kingston would not have been bearable that summer. Not after David's arrival.

David had arrived at Simon's dorm during exam time. Simon hadn't seen him for almost five years, nor had he heard much about him in all that time. He knew David had lived in New York, been in a band, and had claimed in his early letters to their mother to be on the verge of stardom.

Returning from his sedimentology exam, Simon opened the door to his room, the same one he had occupied since his arrival at Queen's, to find David asleep on the bed. At first glance he took in the canary-yellow shirt, the messy, tied-back dreadlocks, the prominent forehead. A stuffed-to-bursting leather bag sat on the floor beside a black jacket thrown over a set of bongo drums. Recognising the glistening scar across the cheek turned his shock to confusion. Simon stared, listening to the steady rise and fall of his brother's breathing before closing the door. Not knowing what to do, he went to the cafeteria for dinner.

When he returned to the room, David was awake, sitting on the bed talking and drinking beer with Kelly, a co-ed from down the hall.

"Welcome, welcome, bro, come and fire one with us," David said as got up and held out a bottle of beer. Simon hesitated, but David reached for his hand and cupped it around the bottle, giving them both a gracious shake and offering half a smile. Simon didn't drink; he just waited, looking at David for some kind of explanation. David shifted his eyes and sat back down.

"Canadian beer's not like the piss in America, man, It's got some bite. Not a bad place you' livin' in Simon." David reached into his bag and pulled out a pack of cigarettes.

"What about New York?" Simon asked finally, as he pulled out the chair from his desk and sat down facing David and Kelly.

"Too expensive," Kelly said, already, as it seemed, aligned with David, who shook out a cigarette and offered one to her.

"You're not going back?" Panic tinged Simon's voice.

"Ah, what for, New York will always be there. Time to try something else. Headed to Toronto. Thought I'd drop in here." David lit Kelly's cigarette and then his own, and looked around the room, at Kelly, but never directly at his brother.

Simon could tell that, as usual, there was more to the story than David was letting on. David looked smaller and wider, but his light still blazed. "*Hol' de light fuh de devil to see* . . ." Simon could hear MacKenzie. He felt a jaundiced twitch in his groin again.

David didn't leave Kingston right away, as Simon had expected. He stayed, sleeping on Simon's floor that first night, then coming and going as he met and made friends among the students who were fascinated by this outsider that had appeared in their dorm. Simon worried that he would be brought to task for David's presence, but no one ever raised the issue with him. In a few days, David met more people than Simon had in his three years at Queen's. Encouraged initially by Kelly, David sang for them and played his drums, charming them with his accent, with his stories of clubs in New York, with things about a wider world that they wanted to feel a part of. An ever-shifting group, mostly female, many of whom Simon had known only by sight, would sit in his room drinking beer and smoking dope.

With one exam left to write, Simon had to go to the library to do his studying. Stratigraphy was stripped of any meaning by David's presence, his ringing laugh, and his easy abandon of all the corners that Simon had always found himself tucked into. David made friends with the cashmere girls, talked philosophy with the artsies down the hall, and was setting to tremble the house of cards of Simon's life. Simon struggled to concentrate, and would stay at the library until it closed, reading about rock formations. He would meander back to Morris Hall, killing as much time as possible, and when he arrived he'd hear David's laugh, a laugh that was not exhausted or forgetful; it contained the same ring of possibility it always had. Simon chose to sleep in the lounge to avoid the all-night scene that now made his room the most popular on the floor.

It was soon obvious that David had fallen for Kelly, whom he found capricious and complicated. "Like a garden maze," he said to Simon. "I've never met anyone like her before." The only daughter of a wealthy New England family, Kelly had chosen a

Canadian university in spite of her parents' wishes for an Ivy League education, and was known for her intensity and her commitment to the film studies department, which was just getting off the ground at Queen's. David was lost, waiting every afternoon for her after exams. He told Simon he loved the circles of her mind, which brought a part of him alive. "She wants to taste every flavour of the universe." They would talk for hours, and giggle, David becoming more vulnerable, Kelly increasingly flirtatious and commanding.

"Who would you be, if you had to choose: Scarecrow, Tin man, or Cowardly Lion?" Kelly's sultry voice could be heard through the door.

"Me? Oh . . ." There was silence for a few seconds. "Dorothy."

Kelly burst into hearty laughter. "Oh, come on . . ."

Simon heard movement, and the sound of kissing.

"You're more like the wizard. You . . ."—and then the sound of rustling clothes—"don't need any more tricks," she said almost breathlessly.

Simon turned and went back outside. He was uneasy around them. Simon and his sisters had always found David's will so overwhelming that their first impulse had been to diffuse it, not to encourage it as Kelly was doing. Simon was uncomfortable hearing David talk about the world in metaphors and declare that he finally saw his own complexity mirrored in Kelly. But when alone with Simon, David would quickly grow restless and reserved, and stare out the window agitated unless he had smoked a joint.

On the night of his last exam, Simon returned to his room to find the usual crowd sitting listening to music, laughing, smoking. The pressure of school was finished for another year and he felt himself let go. He joined them, drinking and smoking. His last memory of that evening was of his head flung back against the wall and a girl standing over him holding a joint to his slightly parted lips. She giggled, so did he. He remembers nothing after that.

An insistent pounding woke Simon early the next morning. He sat up, his fogged brain noting that he had been lying on the floor fully clothed. Dragging himself to the door, he opened it to find the dorm warden and a police officer. Confused and suddenly shamed by the stale smoke, Simon whimpered that the stuff hadn't been his; it wasn't his fault. But the men weren't interested. They asked him about David, where he was, why he had been there. The warden was particularly severe: "Who does he think he is?" After accommodating David that week, his voice was edged with a sense of betrayal. Simon had no idea why they were asking these questions, and he had no answers. He looked back into the room; the leather bag and bongos were gone.

The dorm was silent, the few remaining students who had not packed up their belongings into family cars and rented trucks and left for the summer were shut away in their rooms. After he'd showered and changed, Simon was asked to come to the don's apartment. They told him about his brother: how he'd "forced a girl." Kelly. She had screamed and someone had called the police. "That's not possible," said Simon. "He could never have done that." David was in love with her. But his things were gone. No, he didn't know where his brother was living. No, the visit hadn't been announced. *Forced a girl . . . Forced a girl . . .* Language failed him. Simon could only shake his head. They asked him again if he knew where his brother had gone. Kelly wasn't pressing charges, but they wanted to get to the bottom of the incident. Simon sat silent, stunned, feeling sick and deceived.

He went to his room and slid under his covers. He slept, dreamless, waking the next day and booking a ticket to Barbados. Even now he can remember David's face, just before he passed out that night, looking alert and content from a week in which his essence had been duly acknowledged.

Faye dials the operator for the time. 12:14 A.M. She hangs up, then picks up the receiver and calls again, just to be sure. 12:15 A.M. *Click.*

In the days following the night of whores and angels, Faye waited for Simon to call. She wanted to speak with him, to ask him to meet her, just to talk, or to have him trace patterns on her back once more. Finally, she tracked down David's number through Christine. When she finally worked up the nerve to call, it was David who answered the telephone, and Faye was tempted to hang up. He was a raspy note, and she wanted Simon's clear bell. Eventually, she spoke. David's voice brightened in recognition. His brother wasn't in, he said, but why didn't she drop by, Simon would be back soon.

"My brotha tells me you're a musician too," David said after Faye had settled on the couch.

"Well, not much any more."

"How's that?"

"I haven't had a chance to play much in the last while."

"You good?"

"Not really . . ." She looked at the door, hoping Simon might appear with the turn of her head.

"Mmmm," David let out suspiciously. He rolled a joint and put a tape into the cassette player. "You don't find that hard?"

"What?"

"Not playing."

"No, not really," she lied, shifting slightly, gently patting a cushion.

"But man, it's the only way to find the thing we're lookin' for."

"And what's that?"

"Not a clue, darlin', NOT . . . A . . . CLUE!" He chuckled then ran his tongue over his top lip. "But I know we long for something. Not like wanting sex, man, not the same."

He began to speak of longing like a curse. Longing that was like the pull of warmer climes on migrating birds, or the inexorable flow of a river to the ocean. A kind of homesickness that had nothing to do with place. "When will it stop?" he asked, staring right through her with dark eyes that had no distinguishable pupils. She had no answer.

"You ever heard Nina Simone sing 'Wild as the Wind'?"

"Mm, mm," she said, shaking her head.

"It's the kind of sound that stretches out to tek you in. Unzips you . . . I could play it—"

"No, don't," she threw out, stopping him before he got up, somehow afraid of what she'd hear.

"Whatever, darlin'," he said with a shrug as he eased back into the armchair.

He told her about the feeling in New York, of brushing up against his own vibration, grazing his soul on music that might rescue him. But even New York could afford no place for him. Failure waited for him on every corner, challenging him to be only his skin. He sold things to pawn shops: tape recorders and cameras stolen by people he barely knew, for money that would feed him every two days. He auditioned for bands that advertised in *The Village Voice* or on bulletin boards in bars. He found a few other musicians to start a band, but the money never came. He worked as a busboy, a delivery boy, a boy Friday—all, as he said, "jobs wid boy attached . . . not for men . . . small, small, small, all over again, jus' like at home. At least in Barbados everywhere you look there is colour. Colour as thick as . . ." he searched, "as forgetting."

"And why don't you go back there?" she asked.

"Don't know, really. Not ready to be forgotten just yet."

He was already doing better here in Toronto. He wanted to live in a song, but he couldn't stay there forever, couldn't sing all day. He wondered again when it would stop, all this longing, a throbbing pain like the aching bones he'd had as a growing child. It had only recently occurred to him that this yearning, like a teasing taste on his tongue, would be with him forever— until he died.

Half suspecting David of fibbing that Simon was on his way, Faye finally screwed up the courage to ask where he was.

"He'll be home soon. You stick around. That boy's a bit green, but good through and through. Don't mind his shy-boy way. You wait."

When Simon came home that evening, he and Faye went for a walk in the neighbourhood. She noticed nothing: not the trees, not the houses with tomato plants sprouting in front gardens, not the sound of children up late playing in the street. All she felt was their serried stride and his hand that had fallen to hers, their fingers grazing back and forth. He talked of his sister Maggie, how he had missed seeing her grow up and how he'd one day like children of his own. After that night Faye knew that she would not feel Michael's pull again, that she would stop playing the cello, that she would recover from the tricks music and her heart had played on her. She was falling in love with Simon's dark smile, the deep furrows that formed on his forehead when he was thinking, and his hands, his familiar hands, crisscrossed by fine lines that formed a footpath to overtake Nannerl and to take Faye out of the shadows.

Nannerl Mozart fell ill with typhus of the stomach in September of 1765. She was given the last rites in October, but rallied in November. In November, her brother Wolfgang Amadaeus fell ill with typhus of the stomach and did not recover until the spring of 1766. When Mozart contracted smallpox in October 1767, he recovered just a few days before Nannerl fell ill in November. She regained her health only after a long struggle. In 1784 she married Johann Baptist Franz von Berchtold zu Sonnenburg and had a son, Leopold, named after her father; the father who had overlooked her talents in favour of her brother's.

The only mothers in Mozart's work are Marcella, in *Figaro*, who comes by her child like the Virgin Mary, and the great and primeval mother, *The Magic Flute*'s Queen of the Night: the bravura, soprano, *con anima, con brio, glissando, fortissimo* bitch from hell.

Nannerl gave up music for love and the propriety of an age, but Wolfgang would have both, and would produce many children. Wolfgang, who hated Nannerl's husband, made no effort to see her after she moved to Frankfurt, leaving her marooned from his genius. Faye had felt marooned from her own essence during the entire relationship with Michael. Now her attraction to Simon was grounding her in the world, to the centre of something compelling.

One day she arrived at David's apartment to find Simon waiting for her on the front steps with a look as glad as Christmas. He hugged her tight then guided her over to a corner of the porch where he turned her to face a bicycle. A new, shining, azure Raleigh with a high leather seat and upright handle bars.

"For you," he said simply.

Simon rode beside her on his own bike as they made their way west toward High Park. Here they stopped for ice cream, chatted on the grass, and rode up and down hills that exhausted her legs and lungs. He followed behind as she soared downhill near the pond, nimbly navigating the bumps and cracks in the asphalt. She shot her legs out like aircraft spoilers. Laughing, Simon called after her to be careful. In a moment's backward

glance to gauge his pleasure in her birdspeed, she failed to spot
a fallen branch and had no time to skirt it. The bike shot out
from beneath her and she skidded across the pavement. Searing
pain along her thigh. Simon was beside her immediately and
held her, fussed over her, making sure she was all right. She
barely felt the stinging at her elbow, which Simon examined
with concern. He gathered her up in his arms, brushed her off,
righted her bicycle, and walked her over to the shade. She stared
at him, enchanted, and ran her fingers over his perspiring brow.
He took her hand and kissed the fingers where they were
moist. She realised then that it wasn't so much the physical they
shared, but an essence that transcended all the skin, bows, pegs,
fingerboards, strings—all the sensations and sounds she'd ever
known. It terrified her, but she knew she would concentrate on
love, on hands, on salt if he wanted her to.

When Phillip and Francie greeted him at the airport in
Barbados, Simon cried. Not with the happiness of being home,
but with an awkward shame. He hugged Phillip, who, shorn of
his dreadlocks, he almost didn't recognise. Simon wiped his eyes,
stepped back and smiled, then rubbed Phillip's cropped hair.

"Tryin' wid myself," Phillip said self-consciously.

Hugging Francie, Simon noticed a difference in her—a glow
that could only have come from love—so he teasingly asked her
how Lance the Romance Man was looking after her. Had he
crawled out of his book to sweep her off to the Riviera yet?
She answered by pulling Phillip to her side, grinning. Simon
looked at Phillip, who, with a sweep of his hand, mimed a
symbol of the inevitable that flowed from heart to head.

In the back seat of the car, Simon stared out the window.
The island challenged his absence as they drove past new hotels,

a Kentucky Fried Chicken, new plazas, more fast food. Congestion was blossoming, and Simon rubbed his chin anxiously, trying to absorb the changes taking place in the 160 square miles of this tiny country. When they arrived in Christ Church, he noted that the Garden now had a neighbouring condominium development. Accra beach was smaller, eroded and more crowded, and Phillip referred to it as Rockley Beach for some reason. They pulled into the beach's car park to get a view of the sea and bathers. Simon saw the familiar sign and its renowned misspelling—"Felicia's hair brading at Accra Beach" —and was comforted. A flush, homecoming fever, came over him as Phillip turned into Garden Gap. He cried when he saw his mother, father, Maggie, and MacKenzie waiting at the gate to Willowdale. Maggie had grown tall, and now dwarfed her parents. In the distance, Simon saw Best, nodding with a serious, friendly welcome as he dug in the hibiscus bed.

Best's eyes followed Francie as Phillip cupped the curve of her back to usher her through the gate. He lowered his head and dug the shovel deeper into soil, his heartache as red as the hibiscus blooms, as dark as the veins that fed them. *When a man loves a woman* . . . Simon remembered Best's illustrated love notes and felt the breeze that blew them far out of reach, the distance that love would have had to travel between an illiterate gardener and the romance-injected imagination of his sister. Best was a servant. As though he'd just noticed, Simon was suddenly embarrassed. He quickly went inside.

"If you eat labba and drink creek wata', you'll always go back to Guyana to sit beside the Demerara River," Edwin had said to Simon on trips through the dry northern region of Barbados. He seemed to regret the island's thirsty cane fields when compared to the deep river beds of the Guyana interior. As the whole family sat at the elaborate lunch prepared for Simon's arrival, Edwin spoke about his recent trip to Guyana.

His intention had been to stay in Barbados only until the political climate in Guyana stabilised, and this visit had been to see if it was possible to return for good.

"I ain' neva goin' back to that place!" he said, with a firm shake of his head. He had seen his great experiments fail because of bad management and starvation. The zebus and Santa Gertrudis cattle he had bred were hungry twisted torsos of bone, skin hanging from them like molasses dripping from the lip of a jar. "The Guernseys have been inbred to a stupor, and they can barely produce a few drops of milk each day. And any butter you get from them separates and fizzles if you try to pasteurise it. Those breeders—"

Simon saw him glance up at MacKenzie and knew that his father's disappointment with Guyana had forged a closer bond between them. Edwin changed the subject. "Well, there's enough to keep me busy here in any case. Swine fever again. Always something," he murmured as he took the plate Mackenzie had set down before him. "The horses at the track," he said, shaking his head and dolloping mashed yam onto his plate, "No one is takin' any notice of the number of sprains we get on that turf and yet they go ahead and call the races. The owners are stubborn as hell." There was resignation in his voice, complaining rather than championing a cause as he had done in his prime.

Grace offered Simon more flying fish. "Did Francie tell you her news?" she asked. Simon raised his eyebrows and turned to look at his sister.

"We're getting married," Francie burst out, as though the sentence had been unbearable as a secret. She rubbed Phillips arm briskly. Simon looked at his friend who stared into his plate with a smirk.

"You old dog," Simon teased, then raised his glass. "That's great news." Phillip looked up at his friend with a smile, raised his own glass and nodded. The two drank a toast to each other.

"When's the big day, then?" Simon asked.

"Next summer, so that we can have everyone here. Because," Grace paused. "Because that's not all the news," she continued with pride. "Maggie is going to do her O-levels in England next year. She's ahead of the rest of her class, and we decided it would give her an advantage, since she wants to be a doctor."

Simon was overwhelmed. Everyone was looking at him to gauge his reaction to all this news, but he was struck by the sweep of time, the only words coming to him—*forced a girl*—he couldn't speak.

"Don't worry, Simon," Maggie jumped in, unaware of the relief it gave him, "I doubt I can beat your scores, so your reputation is safe," she joked.

"Ya'll leave the boy alone. He's barely had a chance to catch himself after the flight," said Edwin as he pushed his chair back from the table. When Simon took his plate to the sink, MacKenzie held his face in both of her hands and looked right through him, asking: "You fine enough, boy?"

She was direct, but not judgmental. Her cheeks bulged into a smile after the question. But when he didn't answer her, she resorted to her aphorisms: "In a multitude of words transgression is not lacking, but he who restrains his lips is prudent." She could always read whatever heaviness was hiding inside him.

During the visit, Simon told no one about what had happened in Kingston with David—not even Phillip, with whom he spent long days on the beach. Phillip answered Simon's first questions with words. He had cut off the dreadlocks he'd cultivated over the last few years because he was working in the tourism industry now, and he'd discovered that people treated him coolly with his locks, and made it harder to earn a living. He worked in the evenings as a desk clerk at one of the new hotels. He liked the evening shift, since—he broke into mime—the people were mostly drunk and less demanding; he had less need to speak.

"And the hocus-pocus? Astrology—all that shite?"

Phillip mimed a *no way*. He smiled then drew his hand from his forehead to his chin, unfolding a serious look.

The two friends spent most of the rest of their visit in a silence that was a comfort to them both. A return to boyhood. For Phillip, it allowed him to communicate in mime again. For Simon it was a relief from the three words that grated on his brain.

Simon decided to take a drive, and arrived at Phillip's house without notice.

"Get in," he said through the car window when Phillip came out to the driveway. Phillip hopped in eagerly. They drove towards the east coast. Phillip pointed to a new building that housed a wind-surfing club and motioned for Simon to pull in. Simon waited in the car while Phillip got out to speak to the man in attendance. Simon heard them discussing a package deal for hotel guests, and he noted Phillip's new manner. He was business-like. In touch, on call. His speech was fluid, practised and precise. He had the same thespian quality as always, but in a brand new role.

Their next stop was a rum shop. Phillip frowned at the TV blaring in the corner. He mimed his distaste for American soap operas, but said that Francie was addicted to them. "*Like sand through the hour glass . . . so are the days of our lives.*" Simon was happy to know that his sister's passion for romance had not waned.

"Barbados is changing," Phillip said suddenly.

"Up close and far away," Simon agreed, but he wasn't entirely sure if Phillip had meant it as a good or bad thing. After a few more sips of his Banks beer Simon said: "Let's go. One more stop."

They arrived at Ragged Point Lighthouse and parked the car. Phillip looked questioningly at his friend, but Simon just headed down the path. Turning toward the cliff on the way down, he was hoping to catch a glimpse of Spider, but he almost tripped when he saw the chattel house in shambles, abandoned and storm-torn. The mattress that jutted out from the front door was shredded, picked at, it seemed, by hungry creatures. Simon spotted the articulated neck of the desk lamp that had hovered over the bed. The left wall of the house had toppled, leaving the tattered roof slanting like a leaky tent. A lump moved up Simon's throat.

When they reached the beach, Simon decided to run. He ran, up and down the beach, sweating furiously, while Phillip gazed out to sea. Simon tried to run back the years, to run off a feeling of having lost something in order to gain something else much less certain. Exhausted, he motioned to his friend that they should get on their way. Phillip led the way as the sun started to dip behind the cliff. Half-way up, Simon turned toward the sea and saw that they had come. One, two, then three, diving for fish with military precision, but this time there were only a few—not the massive hungry flock he had seen as a child. Just a trickle of lonely pelicans. He looked up along the shore and saw a new hotel in the cliffs—with winding stairs leading from the terrace across the rocks and down to the sea. Beach umbrellas flapped in the breeze, and a few tourists—not a common sight on that part of the coast—collected shells near the rocks. The pelicans continued to dive, but by then the light had almost disappeared. Simon walked quickly to meet his friend at the car, his thoughts as layered as limestone.

Grace knew that David had visited Simon, since she had been the one to give him the address, but she held herself back from asking Simon questions. Instead she watched him anxiously when he spoke of Kingston, hoping news would slip out without her prying. When she finally raised the subject near the end of his stay, Simon said that, yes, he'd seen David, but that he'd left quickly, probably for Toronto where he'd had an audition.

When his two-week vacation was over and he had to return to Kingston to work as a lab assistant for his seismology professor, Simon was almost relieved: the swallowed words . . . *forced a* . . . had become indigestible. But returning to Kingston would not be easy.

MacKenzie cooked enough flying fish and dolphin to last him a week and packed it carefully, hiding it in layers of plastic bags inside Simon's suitcase.

"Neva mind ya Guyanese labba and creek wata boy, you eat me fish and you gonna come back to Barbados."

It was one of the only trips into Canada where Simon has had his bags searched by Customs. Although the food was cooked, the Customs official confiscated MacKenzie's fish with a snarl.

Simon gets up from his desk to pace the cold floor of the basement, very slowly, one step following the other like the opening and closing of a valve—a heart valve pumping a little blood in, letting a little blood out. Step after balanced step.

He has never eaten labba nor drunk creek water. He wonders about returning anywhere where the leaves do not die, the ground does not freeze up, and the sky does not turn pewter with the threat of ice.

CHAPTER 6

Water

Faye opens the window wide and October spits a leaf at her with its frigid breath. She stares into the dark as cold wind from the east washes over her face and shoulders. A twig blows into the studio, glancing off her head. She has to think now, to put this part together, to unspool guilt and to wind it through the night. Her eyes follow the shadowy form of a raccoon as it scampers over the flat roof of a garage that backs onto the alley beyond their small garden. She stands motionless, feeling goosebumps rise on her arms and skin tighten at the corner of her eyes. She can't push it away anymore. A dry leaf spins into her shoulder, another at her chest. And another. *Whip, whip, whip. Penance.* She counts aloud . . . *one, two, three, four, five, six, seven* . . .

Seven. Seven years. David killed himself seven years after she met him. It's been seven years since the night Simon traced patterns on her back, willing her to guess the shape of a salt crystal. It was the moment when the universe expanded to include pictures—seventh heaven. Seven: seven wonders of the world; seven continents; seven deadly sins; seven brides for seven sons; a song, their song, about seven seconds away; seven digits to a telephone number; they live across from a Seven-Eleven. Seven years, they say, is the length of love.

Simon and Faye decided to move in together about year after they met, and found a one-bedroom flat over a fish store on Bloor West, not far from where David was living. Before that they struggled for space. Faye's studio was too small; David's apartment was always buzzing with people. Soon after the night of whores and angels, Simon began to look for an apartment of his own. His stay with his brother had always been intended as

temporary, neither of them entirely comfortable with the reap-
pearance of family patterns. And tension. Simon would stay out
long past tiredness or would prefer to sleep at Faye's studio
rather than confront nights of music and improvisiation among
David's friends and girlfriends. The few times Faye stayed
overnight made them all uncomfortable. In her presence the
brothers seemed wary. David would dwell on stories of Simon's
boyhood obsession with cricket, or would refer to his scholastic
achievements in reference to their father. Some mornings it felt
as if David and Simon talked to each other through Faye, told
her things that they would not say directly to each other,
leaving her confused and at times conflicted.

Simon found a place he could afford in Willowdale. The
apartment was spartanly furnished with his few belongings, and
Faye made it a point to bring him the necessary odds and ends:
dishes bought at a yard sale, a radio, candles for his dining table.
When the weather was good, she'd ride her bicycle to see him
after work, all the way to the north end of the city, and there
would fall asleep immediately, sometimes even before they'd
made love. Sleep, sleep, sleep . . . a dainty surrender, pitchless,
rhythmless, a long silent breath . . . *hush, hush . . . dolce, dolce . . .*
voce velata. A gift. They joked that sleep would fatten her, that
like dough set aside to rise overnight she'd swell into puffy mid-
thirties and have to be baked. She knew that she was just
catching up. When they made love she felt fragments of herself
clinging to his centre and shedding from her insides so that
sometimes it hurt. The feeling troubled her. After a time she
stopped going to Willowdale as frequently. Terrified at what
their closeness meant, fearing another dissolving, she drew back
from intimacy. The phone became where she was most
comfortable with Simon. Seven digits: *one, two, three, four, five,*
six, seven . . . a combination of numbers that alone had meaning
among all the digits dialled during her day.

Her telemarketing solicitation turned feeble, and she found

herself pausing before her pitch, just listening to the breathing that followed the "Hello?" at the other end of the line. In that moment she could imagine transmitting her message through vibration alone, the urgency of her breath. She'd call Simon when he wasn't at home, simply to hear the phone ringing, and then convinced him to get an answering machine so that she could hear his voice when her need grew strong—a music that replaced what she wasn't playing. She tried to remain independent, clinging only to his voice at first, leaving messages that would invite him to phone her so that they could make love over the telephone. Simon was an answer to a question she had been posing most of her life: *Who will hear me when I'm silent?* At first he was dismayed by her retreat, but when she explained that she was vanquishing the past, he appeared to understand.

Occasionally, she visited her father, who now lived alone in a small apartment. He had taken nothing with him from the house he'd moved to from Ireland, the one where he'd married, raised two children by proxy, and to where he'd returned from the racetrack to find his wife dead in the armchair. All the browning furniture in the apartment had come with it: rented sooty fingerprints on cupboard doors; rented oily head-marks on the armchair; rented mould around the bathtub tiles. He still went to the racetrack regularly, and his accent glittered through heavy false teeth when he spoke of his small gains. They had little to say to each other—Faye, weaving, weaving for belonging with the sharpness of Simon pushing her through, but her father, his face heavily creased, was so far in the past . . . *reach, reach* . . . that she thought she might fall. But when his hands shook while pouring tea, she felt like his daughter. Just like him, avoiding traces of the past, inheriting new marks, someone else's. His hands, too, resembled hers. Like Simon's, all similar. So many hands, shaping her, pointing her back to herself.

On the streetcar home after a short visit with her father, she plunged into thought. As she gazed blankly at passing storefronts and billboards one caught her attention. Although she'd seen the silly advertisement for car tires many times before, the image of a baby plunked in the middle of a tire, smiling happily, safely, provoked a burst of fear. She showed up at Simon's apartment unannounced and proposed that they move in together. When he agreed with alacrity she set about finding them a place downtown, and perused the classified section of newspapers for a new job, something filling—like fluid to top up a hollow cactus, to make it stand straight and independent . . . *To reach . . . reach . . .*

They found a one-bedroom apartment over a fish store in the west end. Her cello she put in its case and slid it into a closet. Her bow she hung like a piece of art on the wall. She left her telephone solicitation job to work as a clerk at Sam the Record Man.

At first she was accosted by row upon row of discs and tapes with dollar figures—$12.99, $15.99, $21.99—scrawled in black marker across an artist's face. Everything reduced, a miniature evocation of the artist—on sale. She was assigned to the classical section to serve customers, stock shelves, and assist in orders. Bringing stacks of CDs from the stockroom, she had to pass through the pop section. Returning to her station after the hopping of pop felt like stepping on to a cloud. The air was softer. She spent a year there, just listening, avoiding cello pieces, and discovering virtuoso dance music from the 1350s. Plague music. Music to dance to while all around are dying.

In Boccaccio's *Decameron*, ten young noblemen and women of Florence withdraw for ten days from the city, where the plague rages, to find refuge in a country house and entertain themselves with singing, dancing, and storytelling. Courtly love, erotic wit. The plague in Europe brought death to more than twenty-five million people. In death something was born. Boccaccio transformed the vernacular and popular songs of the day to the level of art, and his story set to dance music became hymns to joy in the *Il chominciamento di gioia.* Faye began to dance, to stamp, hop, and trot during the *istanpitta, salterello,* and *trotto.* Through these steps she leached away the hormones she had been ingesting over the years of baby hope with Michael. They were replaced with the rhythmic faith that if one could dance away from the ravages of plague, one could dance toward any life.

She remained cautious, trying to keep all the parts in place, touching them from time to time to see if they would echo, hollow, and sometimes they did, so she'd trot again . . . *trotto, trotto.*

All prancing was a delicate step forward. She danced for Simon, who would not, though the damage inflicted by the trap was healing, his limp barely noticeable except when negotiating stairs. She threaded her love for him, preparing to weave it through everything she had ever known. She learned to see in new ways—to anticipate the things Simon saw. She learned that island people have an innate sense of gloom, a gene for shipwreckedness found only in those surrounded entirely by water, which makes them at once hopeful—"*is that a sail? Do you see movement in the distance?*"—and yet forlorn—"*save this piece of driftwood; it comes from 'out there'; mark this spot with it, a mark of our existence, because others will come after, when we are gone . . . one day . . . they will come . . .*" Simon was a marker, and an observer of passages, of the earth in time, the slow time of geology. There was something under every surface, and Faye learned to mark a moment the way the sea marks a cliff: slowly, purposefully, invisibly assimilating it.

They did their best to be a family, small yet extended, and would have the occasional night out with David, who was then playing steadily in a band that performed at bars around the city and on campuses throughout Ontario. Simon liked to hear the band play, and it was only during those times that Faye could sense the brothers' communion, a connection that originated in rhythm and pulse. She knew that for Simon even the strained contact with David kept him from feeling utterly marooned among strangers.

David made friends wherever he went. After a string of groupies and music vampires, as he called them, he met Justine. She was a tall, beautiful woman with long blonde hair and delicate bones. Her mouth was wide and full, a bulging pocket of teeth. Faye thinks it was the mouth that brought them together; their matching mouths. Justine lived north of the city, in the bedroom community of Newmarket. *To market to market to buy a fat* . . . David had met her when the band had played there one hot summer weekend. His love was instant, he told Faye at dinner when Justine went to the washroom: "Like fire in de groin," he grinned. Faye was skeptical of David's commitment. He was a raft, drifting if untethered. Needing the tether but also the tide. Justine moved into his apartment on Shaw Street a few weeks after they met. They married a month later, with Faye and Simon as witnesses at the courthouse. Their short honeymoon was spent in Barbados.

In the next year there was a baby girl they named Rita. Feeling the financial squeeze, David took a part-time job as a security guard, but he continued to focus on promoting the band across the country. Justine often asked Faye to babysit so that she could attend the band's sessions. Simon would sit with Faye as she fed and changed baby Rita, both of them watching her as she slept, reacting to her stirrings, ready to comfort her. Family: front and centre. Faye's yearnings returned. Justine gave her Chinese herbs and put her on a regime of primrose oil, vitamin E, selenium, folic acid, and it was then that she would furiously wedge Simon inside her two or three times a week. When he touched her it felt like truth. Simon would be overwhelmed, ravished by her energy and belief that their boiling love could make a new life, and he'd hesitate at moments that didn't seem truly intimate. He'd stop her and hold up her head,

stare straight into her eyes, and say: "Wait, wait . . . come here."
Then he'd kiss her, slowly and deeply, rubbing her temples,
massaging all parts of her so that she'd relax. Then, when she'd
gone over the edge, he'd dive into her with a veracious hope
that pierced all the lies she'd ever known. Explosion. A big bang
like the beginning of time. She'd rub her belly, sure of creation.

Nothing. And still nothing.

Their days over the fish store continued, the odours rising
in the morning, diminishing in the late afternoon. Having
explored and listened to all the music that was of interest to her,
Faye moved on from Sam's to administrative work with a small
orchestra, where the days paced themselves with the preparations of plans, schedules and reports, bills and budgets—days of
quiet, solitary work mixed with periodic flurries of intense
activity. When the government grant for her position was not
renewed, she remained at home, reading newspapers and mysteries. David and Justine had another baby, another girl they
named Miriam. Time ticked very slowly.

In the apartment next door, the emotional peaks of a
Russian woman, her infant, and a come-and-go husband could
be heard through the wall. The baby was sick and cried night
and day. Faye called on the woman a few times, to see if she
could help with the child, but the mother refused to take it to
the hospital. From her contradictory and complicated explanations in broken English, Faye suspected the woman was in the
country illegally and feared being deported. The baby cried and
cried. Faye read books. Neighbours complained, but the baby
continued to cry. Faye marked her days by the rise and fall of
snapper, sole, herring and sea bass, and the punctuating screams
from next door.

On hot afternoons, when no amount of incense could
disguise the pungency in the apartment, she would walk to the
park to sit under a tree and read more mystery and adventure
novels, waiting for Simon to come home from work. She would

then convince him to spend the evening in a café or air-conditioned movie to get away from the smell.

Faye closes the window. She shakes off the leaves that have tangled in her hair. Shivering, she walks to the bathroom and turns on the tap in the tub. She sprinkles drops of lavender and rosemary oil into the water, undresses, and waits, goosebumped and quivering, for the bath to fill. The water is hot as she slides in, so hot that she gasps, but she braves it, slowly submerging herself. Slowly, slowly . . . an inch at a time . . . *aaahhhh*. The sound of Simon . . . *aaahhhhh, so it's you . . .*

Simon had long before given up the idea of fieldwork, having spent two miserable years in the bush in northern Alberta. She knows that he surprised himself, and his whole family, by quitting his job with the largest petroleum company in the country. On hot summer nights she and Simon lay naked on top of the bedsheets while he described the feeling of insects on his skin. He had been helicoptered into black-fly-infested land he felt nothing for, a land he was sure would absorb him like carrion. He described the other men, angry and subject to an internal purring that spurred them to fight. The skirmish-ready stance of the rig workers, he told her, arose from their need to touch something that wasn't rock, and they would easily succumb to angry flesh. He returned to Barbados to try to live there permanently, to be near the sea, but something failed him there too.

He's never really spoken to her about it, but she knows that something elemental had rejected him, or him it. His time on the island was like a grafting of skin that didn't take. He returned to Toronto and stayed with David, who found him the job at the meat-packing plant. By the time they met, Simon already seemed haunted somehow. He worked hard, never complaining, just looking whipped as he climbed the stairs amidst the stench of haddock. Their life continued in that way: Faye reading and reading, with the occasional temp job, and, without her noticing, Simon's inner ache becoming his skin.

Her tenacity for trashy books gave out in the middle of a true story about a young man in Italy who planned the brutal murder of his parents because he wanted his inheritance without waiting for them to die. His friends helped him to beat and stab his mother and father with knives and blunt objects. Italian youth, polled on their opinion of the young men, supported their actions, some calling them modern heroes. She dashed the book in the garbage. *Tock, tock, tock* . . . time hobbled on.

Faye scrubs her legs with a cloth. The water is cooler now. It's late, almost three, and he's still in the basement. They've kept the music going, taking turns to put in another CD, careful to avoid each other. But now she hears Simon in the kitchen. Sounds of bottles. Rum? Will he try numbness? She knows that tonight she must think and think and think before the sun comes up. David has left his body, but not hers. He's churning up his own story, and tonight they're tossing in its wake. *Simon, dear Simon, if you touch me again I will know the truth* . . .

Sugar cane was brought to Barbados in 1627 by Henry Powell, leader of the first colonists, who ventured to the Essequibo River to collect plant materials and to solicit the help of Amerindians in teaching settlers tropical agriculture. It was later introduced on a large scale using plants from Brazil. Fatter, sweeter-stemmed cane came via the French and English in the eighteenth century. The idea of improving the cane's sweetness through propogation began to take hold, and its fertility soon became apparent. The finest seeds were sown throughout the island. And then RUM: the glorious "kill-devil" liquid—called rumbullion or rumbustion—known as the "skimmings of the coppers" because it was made from the scum that came to the surface when cane juice was boiled. The molasses was boiled again, fermented, distilled, then, magically: rum.

Simon pours until the glass is half full. *"Kill-devil always has de wrong effect . . . dat not to kill de devil heself, but to let he rise up."* MacKenzie's voice again. She would warn them all of the evils of drink, especially David, who had begun drinking early and regularly with his teenage friends.

Barbados has some of the finest rums in the world— strong—and if he drinks it straight, on ice, he can begin to smell something like soil, a deep, burnt humus smell that has granulated into the earth that grows cane. It has a scent of fossil from the reef that caps the island. Dead sea creatures in his glass, swimming in ice, squirming down his belly, heating it, then softening the space behind his eyes. It relieves the weight. He hasn't yet cried. *If I cry the tears will freeze on my cheeks. Not enough salt. I am bereft of salt. I will not let myself cry.*

When he went back to Kingston after the embarrassment with David and Kelly, Simon quietly completed his final year of studies, graduated with *cum laudae* status, and tried to get a job in a precious-metal mine in northern Ontario. In the hierarchy of jobs for geological engineers, the hard-rock positions were the most coveted. Many of Simon's fellow graduates were the sons or relatives of mine owners, and Simon sensed his exceptional grades could not compensate for his lack of connections or his pending residency status. He was overlooked for every available position. The tight-knit clan of mine owners excluded him. With encouragement from his father he took a far less prestigious job in the soft-rock sector with an Alberta petroleum company immediately on graduation.

Singly, black flies are almost imperceptible, but in numbers they form an inescapable net. Throughout the days of that first month in the Alberta bush he'd wriggle to escape, hopelessly trying to beat them off. During the night their presence was replaced by wind and vague animal cries, or an intense silence in which Simon imagined hearing the exhalations of the land itself. He trained as a seismic geologist; his job involved analysing the signals picked up by geophones—instruments that register the echo of dynamite underground—to help discern the pattern of the earth's strata. A hard layer beneath a soft one meant the probable presence of oil, but sometimes the sounds were deceiving and drilling could lead merely to salt water, the remnant of an ancient sea bed. The accuracy of his work was crucial, and he diligently interpreted the computer data and made maps of the strata, calculating depths, mass, and weight, all without pleasure.

Most of the other new graduates he worked with were seasoned outdoorsmen—experienced hikers, campers, canoeists, hewers of wood. Simon's boy scout experience in Barbados had no bearing in that deep northern bush. In the first month he was sore and tired, in the second stronger and yet more fatigued as the heat and mosquitoes of July sapped and sucked what salt was left in his blood. He was lost in deep woods, frightened and the most alone he'd ever felt in his life . . . *perhaps until now* . . .

Simon knew he wanted to get away on his first night, as he listened to owls calling to each other, wondering, *who? . . . who?* He wondered with them. His desire to escape grew as the months wore on and he found himself secretly wishing they'd drill down to an ancient sea and he could revive himself with salt water. In the Edmonton winter, when his work shifted indoors to the sorting and application of data in the company's head office, he was not relieved but further dismayed by a feeling that his skin was growing scales. The dryness of the minus-thirty-degree cold and the stale office air caused a constant itching that even the blackflies had not prepared him for. His decision was final after two years, when in late June he stepped into the animal trap that broke his foot, and he was sent to the nearest hospital. He didn't return to the camp. He took on paperwork at the head office, learning to program the computer that spit out the geophone data. But several months later, with his bank account brimming, he quit. He bought a ticket to Toronto, where he stayed with David and waited for his foot to mend.

He finishes his rum quickly, then pours another. He hears MacKenzie's voice: "*I know you gon' deny it, boy, gon' deny it three times or maybe more . . .*" He gulps down the second rum.

Using the number his mother had given him, Simon called David from Edmonton and told him when he would be arriving. David picked him up at the airport in a borrowed car, and they drove to a bar where they each ordered a rum and soda and raised their glasses to each other without their eyes meeting. He can feel the same tightness in his chest, keeping the words *forced a girl* still locked in his gullet. It had been more than four years since they'd seen each other. They stayed away from the subject of Queen's and talked instead about Guyana, about childhood picnics at the seawall. Old family jokes.

Simon passed his days in David's apartment and rarely went out. He lodged there for a month, slowly resolving to go back to Barbados to build there a place for himself outside of time— a place preserved in salt. He learned of international organisations doing research into the effects of sea level change in Barbados. McGill University had established the Bellairs Institute, a marine biology unit on the St. James coast, and researchers were delving into the deposition and diagenesis of carbonate sediment in a reef environment, studying the effects of changes in sea level in the Pleistocene and Holocene eras. Simon became excited about the possibility of going to Barbados and getting a job; he could do research, surely he could apply the seismic mapping he had mastered in the bush to beneath the sea, to map out beds of coral. He packed his bags.

Phillip picked him up at the newly expanded airport. Package deals had made travel much cheaper, and Barbados was seeing an influx of visitors. In addition to the traditional British, Canadian, and German tourists, the Americans were coming in greater numbers and expanding their investment on the island.

The road from the airport merged with a new highway, but Phillip took a detour to their favourite rum shop, passing by their old school, where, to Simon's surprise, boys were playing basketball in the yard. After firing a rum in silence, they headed to the Garden. They arrived at Willowdale to find Best securing bars to a side window. He looked up at Simon and nodded hello.

Grace emerged from the house and hugged Simon tightly, kissing him three times. The bars, she explained, catching his quizzical look, were being installed because of a spate of armed robberies in the neighbourhood. Simon held tight to her hands and stared into her face. Grace's skin was as smooth as ever, but her eyelids and cheeks had loosened. In turn, Grace searched Simon's face with a tenderness mixed with vague dread, her eyebrows arched, hoping to divine the reason behind her son's return home. Simon picked up his bags quickly and went inside.

He spent a few days just sleeping late before heading off to the lighthouse. Scrambling down the familiar cliff, he noted the difference his injured foot made to his experience of seeing again the small hidden beach at the foot of the rocks. He sat on the beach for awhile, then waded into the surf to his hips. As he waited for the pelicans to arrive he pictured Best's youthful face, the steady nod that he'd given him that seemed to say: "I'm still here," underlining Simon's years of absence. The sea lapped at his waist and the salt air swept his cheeks, a sensation he had always remembered. He searched the sky for the pelicans. He returned to the beach to wait. Nothing. It got dark. He limped his way up the cliff in the early moonlight.

He drove out each day and waited for the birds to arrive and do their dive-bomb act, to acknowledge him. He watched the sky, hopeful. Nothing. More empty waiting. They never came. Three weeks of watching and not a single pelican. He began to understand that they would never return. They had been eroded. He detested the wind that blew hard against the cliff—wind that could erode rock, carry a jet, banish the flight of sea birds. He returned to the Garden in the late afternoons to play cribbage with Phillip. Days bled into one another: sun-soaked days dripping with lethargy.

Phillip endured his silences. Simon felt distanced from his best friend, and even more so from Francie. Phillip and Francie were now married—a wedding Simon had missed while in the Alberta bush—and Francie was fat with their second child. She waddled through the heat in the Garden on afternoon visits, holding their young baby against her bulging second, and moaning: "Dis life gwan kill me—legs g'on wear out and drop me to de ground." She would pout, her lips as swollen as the moment before rain.

Neighbours in the Garden asked Simon, each time they saw him, about his plans. He was constantly compared to Maggie, the other "scholar" in the family, who had set off to England the previous fall to do pre-med at university in Bristol. They all wanted news of his life in Canada.

"The Dragon got a knitted brow," Phillip would tell Simon each time they saw Edwin. His father refused to believe that Simon was home to stay and kept asking him how his foot was healing and when the company would want him back.

Edwin had retired from his private practice and spoke bitterly about news from his colleagues in Guyana. The back-crossing breeding that he had practised—hybrid cattle bred back to thoroughbreds, or F1—was still a viable means of improving stock, but vets were considering new technology. Their work was focussed on high-yield. They practised surrogate breeding, using ordinary commercial cows as surrogate mothers for the embryos of pedigree breeding stock. The cows were given hormones to produce multiple ovulation, then ova were fertilised with sperm from high-quality males, either in the cow or in a test-tube. The embryos were transferred into surrogates. This enabled a cow to produce as many as twenty rather than an average of 3.5 offspring per lifetime. Importation of frozen embryos was also a more economical way of making high-quality breeds available in Guyana. Pedigree stock, his colleagues hoped, would soon be cloned, which would produce large numbers of genetically identical animals with superior meat- or milk-producing capabilities. The threshold of transgenic breeding stood before them: new breeds containing genes from other species would be created to withstand heat and drought. These new genetic manipulations, Edwin noted, would be sterile, ultimately useless to the people. Scientists had forgotten a primary principle of their discipline: it is not true that any creature capable of survival is bound to be physically stable and content.

Edwin would get himself worked up talking about Guyana, and Grace would try to change the subject to calm him. Simon noticed that his father tired more easily, and when he did, the left side of his face would droop, as though blood was slowly being cut off from his visage. Edwin continued to treat the thoroughbreds that visited the Garrison every month. He stayed clear of stud breeding, but was still in demand for sprains, infections, and ticks, and his enthusiasm for spirited, wild horses had not diminished,al though he would return from calls at the racetrack visibly drained.

Grace assures Simon that Edwin's heart and blood pressure are perfectly normal for a man of his age, but when he is tired, as was acutely evident today, a fatigued gravity favours one side of his body. Like Simon, Edwin did not shed a tear at the funeral, but the skin on his left cheek wept in his stead.

Simon walks through the kitchen to the living room, ice cubes tinkling in his full glass. He wonders what his father is thinking now. Does he remember the weight of his own words regarding journeys and anchors in the note to David so many years ago? Would they drag him into regret as he lies awake in the motel with Grace, MacKenzie, Maggie, Phillip, Francie, and his grandchildren all crammed into two rooms? Simon's last trip to Barbados and his father's last trip to Guyana were similar. Unwitnessed changes accused them both of neglect. For both of them, returning home was like denouncement. They had moved on, but home had been abandoned and left to ravages both native and foreign. During the months Simon spent on Barbados trying to imagine a place for himself there, he started to feel himself slipping out of his skin, as though the space between bone and flesh had widened with nothing to fill it up. Home had become a hollow, echoing word. He went back one last time to Ragged Point to look for the pelicans, but still nothing.

Driving back home through St. Phillip, he was aware of the shabby chattel houses that lined the highway. Thin, barefoot children in cut-offs ran in the streets, their mothers hanging out of windows, breasts like loaves of bread cooling on the sills. He tuned in sharply to their poverty, which he had never given much thought to before. He thought of MacKenzie and Best and their bus ride each day from the countryside to the Garden, along with many other servants. MacKenzie's shift, the same one every day, only a few changes through the years, sliding into the crack in her buttocks again, over and over.

He turned the car around, not wanting to go back to the Garden right way. He went farther along the east coast, to Cattlewash and Bathsheba. Very few tourists. He bathed in an Atlantic rock pool from where he could see in the distance the arrow-head tip of the rocks at Pico Tenerife, rocks that had been ironed by the wind, flat on one side, pinched at the tip, an inverted image of a nursed teat of one of the wild dogs that ran the beach. He looked out to sea, lost himself in the surf whose only previous land obstacle had been Africa. His skin felt tighter: salt and belonging. He walked along the beach and picked up pieces of brain coral that mocked his own soggy cerebral mass. He took them back to the car and drove farther north, all the way to North Point, where renovations of an old-time hotel were underway. Around the tip of the island, he passed Speightstown and Holetown and the chic hotels on the St. James coast. As he passed through Bridgetown and on to the Garden, his skin sagged again. The Garden appeared overgrown —hotel apartments, tourist boutiques, and construction in the heat. Home became a craving, not a place. He wanted to run away then, to return to Canada or to go somewhere even farther away—Australia, China—so as to justify the space now echoing between bone and flesh. This was the answer to the puzzle of ageing. It wasn't gravity mixed with time that caused the body's peeling; it was prolonged homesickness. The farther we go from home, from a vital source, the more yearning we put between ourselves and our bodies, the more our skin sags. He returned to Canada six months later, and within weeks had met Faye. With her back to him as he illustrated salt in the space between her shoulder blades, he knew he was not drawing, but tracing what was already there: the fine angles of something absolute.

Faye reaches the living room, wrapped in a towel, in time to see Simon's back as he navigates the stairs with a glass of rum in one hand. His hair, she's sure, has more splotches of grey. Curls like vines crawl about his head, looking for something new to attach themselves to. Wild and forsaken curls. She wants so much to touch them, but instead she turns to check the oak chest in the hall. She opens it. The envelope she hid is still there. She was afraid that in his rummaging through the long night Simon might have come across it. Nothing she knows about

herself can explain why she hasn't given it to him yet; nothing
except fear, which has been her master before. She goes into the
living room to the CD player and tucks *Le Nozze di Figaro* into
the slot; it skates on.

Viennese opera-goers resented *Figaro*. It was the beginning
of Mozart's decline from favour; it insulted the bourgeoisie that
had once hailed him. In the story, a count—a man of breeding
and power—is thwarted by his own servant, who ends up the
victor, and who expresses his confidence in radiant C-major.
The bourgeoisie began to avoid Mozart. Susanna rules over that
opera, projecting reason more than feeling, an unerring
planner, smarter and more calculating than her fiancé.

Faye starts to shiver, so returns upstairs to the bathroom and
runs more hot water into the tub. She puts in more oil . . . *slink,
slink* . . . and slides in again.

It was Faye who found this beautiful cottage on the park in
the Greek neighbourhood, wanting so desperately to get away
from the smells of the fish store and the screams of the neighbours. She'd begun to see patterns of fish appear in oily stains
on the wallpaper. Susanna in F-major: "*Déh, vieni . . .*" Simon
just followed, by then entrenched at the Ministry of Natural
Resources. Seeking some way to get out of the meat-packing
plant, Simon solicited the advice of a former professor at
Queen's. Although overqualified for the position, Simon was of
little threat to the other bureaucrats, and he was granted an
interview because of the professor's connections. He pursued
the position avidly, researching the ministry's mandate, rewriting
his professional profile to fit the prerequisites of the job, and
pulling off an exceptional interview. Within a week he was
signed on, set up, and initiated into the well-worn routine of

office days, earning a living for them—*the beginning of his sorrow, I know, with tonight the cap of that wave.*

She remembers Simon in the first few days in this house, walking through it and his job, this city, like a visitor from the dark, but then he seemed to settle in. Something clicked—some gene of endurance that she could trace to none other than his mother. And Faye returned to telemarketing. Her shifts were short and she'd arrive home early each weekday and wait for Simon to come home. In the silence and freshness of their small house, it was *Figaro* that led the rhythms in her brain. She felt at times to be the scheming Susanna, then the young and tender Barbarina who had hidden resources that would ensure her comfort, resisting the Count, astonishing Figaro. *E cosi, tenerella, il mestiero gia sai di far tutto si ben quel che tu fai? . . . For your tender years you know your business amazingly well!* But then Barbarina loses her tiny ornamental pin for which she sings with such radiance . . . *L'ho perduta* . . . such loss. The loss of so much more than a pin.

Faye rests her head against the back of the tub. She is there now. The flow of memory has come to this. The whole story. She submerges her ears to drown Barbarina's aria, her *perduta*.

It was during that time, when they first moved into the new house, that Justine got pregnant for the third time. David started to panic, wondering how he'd provide for the hungry females in his life on his part-time income as a security guard and with the dwindling revenue from the band. When Vanessa was born, he knew he'd have to give up singing, give up music. He sank into a deep depression. He looked for full-time work, but was unable to find anything. Finally, a friend of Justine's got him a job in a correction facility.

David watched over juveniles doing time. For someone to

"do" time suggested to Faye the requirement of performing a physical act, like doing the rounds, doing a good deed, doing work, not just sitting and waiting in a cell. But perhaps doing nothing is doing time, lost in the physicality of emptiness, the carnality of absence. David would talk to the boys about music, suggest rare recordings they should listen to. He was well-liked, a good guard, and he worked hard to look after Justine and the three girls.

That was three years ago. Things seemed to be settling for everyone, for Faye and Simon in their house, their jobs, for David and his family. Faye worked hard, selling more subscriptions than ever before, spending her income decorating the house: rugs, lamps, wood-and-glass furniture. Cool metals and warm textures side by side. She luxuriated in things she'd been denying herself, and returned to Mozart. She memorized *Figaro*, *Don Giovanni*, and *Cosi fan tutte*. Her cello remained in the closet. In the spring, Simon's parents visited to see their grand-children, David's children.

That summer, she got a call at work from David. She could barely understand what he was saying on the other end of the line. He was in tears, drunk, and he wanted her to meet him somewhere downtown.

"What's wrong?" she asked.

Sniffling. He cleared his throat. "Please, just come."

"Where? Where's Justine?"

"Nobody's anywhere . . ."

"David? Are you there?" She heard his breathing again, and began to panic, thinking he must have been in an accident. "Where are you?"

Arriving at the address she had scribbled down, Faye knocked gently on the door. David opened it to let her in. He had a wild glint in his eyes. He hugged her too hard and ushered her in.

"What's going on?"she asked, calmer, seeing that he hadn't been injured.

He wouldn't look at her, just poured a rum and offered it to her. She sipped. He took up his guitar and started to play. She sat down across the room from him. His voice was weak under a strummed chord: "I'm shrivelling."

The words unbuttoned her. She crossed her legs.

"What do you mean?"she asked, unnerved.

"Like a fruit, left too long in the sun, insides sucked out by heat, moisture taken to give rain . . . rain like drink for the earth, but not the fruit, just shrivelling, too late . . ."

"I don't understand," lied Faye, knowing what he was describing but not wanting to join him there. She looked around at the room's cluttered furnishings, the tattered rugs, the many photographs on the walls and mantle, the wooden masks arranged around the door frame. "Whose place is this?"

"A friend's, from the jail. I couldn't go home. Not to more crying." He gulped rum.

"Tell me."

"She cries, all night long, my little one . . . all night, cause she knows . . . knows better than all of us."

"Knows what, David?" Faye asked more urgently, realising his coherence would soon slip away completely.

"I need to play, that's all. Can't give anything back if it's not comin' in."

Faye stared at the swelling tremolo in his lips and felt her left hand start to shake. She rubbed her thumb along her fingertips, which were smooth, no longer callused from strings.

"There's never enough money," he held back a sob. "I have no choice. But, damn it, she knows, Vanessa knows . . . we'll all be thirsty soon. Her daddy's thirst will suck it out of all of us." He stopped strumming. His head fell back slightly and Faye moved forward as if to catch him, but he grabbed her arm and stared intently at her, trying to focus through the blaze of alcohol.

"You know ...Why don't you say it? Say it to me. If ya can't have the only thing that comes to ya, then what the fuck is there to have." He let go of her arm with a slight shove.

She could feel the inevitable rumbling towards her.

"What is it to be fed from shrivelled fruit?" he said. She didn't answer, and the silence mediated their breathing. Soon he fell asleep.

She didn't leave. Should she have phoned Simon, asked him to come and help his brother? David wouldn't have been able to explain himself to anyone in his family. Only she would know what he meant, as she had since their first encounter: "*All that heavin' and fuckin' at holy air.*"

She stayed and wandered around the apartment, knowing she should get back to the office, but unable to imagine herself anywhere but here, glared at from the empty slits of eyes of the masks on the mantle. No sign of Figaro, of Susanna, of Don Giovanni. She put on albums of groups she'd never heard before —reggae groups, African drum music—and watched David sleeping. One hand was tucked between his leg and the couch, while the other bare arm fell across the white singlet that stretched over his chest, accentuating the arch of his biceps. A gentle shoulder. Skin like a girl's. Long, hefty hands. She smoked, blowing smoke rings and allowing her gaze to linger along the curve of his thigh, down his corduroys, to his indelicate feet. She sipped rum, standing still to watch his breathing. The music was beautiful, split and polyphonic, fragmented and contradictory.

When David woke a half-hour later he was clearer, softer.

"Would you mind getting me a drink of water?" he asked.

When she returned from the kitchen she sat on the couch next to him as he drank. He touched the hand lying on her parched thigh. Her underclothes dissolved. The room sang—the speech of forgotten angels that now turned to them—and she bent her head to his, kissing him as though swallowing an echo, whole and hollow. He turned her over and was on top of her, peeling off his clothes, throwing hers aside, his lips covering the pale territory of her tall cells, his need swimming like a determined fish up and up and up and up into the shower of her recognition.

At first it was fast and omnivorous, but when he was inside he slowed ... *largo, larghetto, larghissimo* ... and opened his eyes. He began to cry and his tears fell on her face, dripping down her cheeks. She tasted one, the tangy smooth gift of water. Almost humming, he said, "you know, I wondered if you were like the ruby slippers ..."

She stayed silent, her face now drenched, crying his tears for him as he pushed himself deep into her.

" ... you have them with you all the time but don't know they're the thing that gets you home ..."

Then ... *allegro allegro* ... more intent, and she found herself on the edge, squirming inside ... *glissando* .... until she burst ... *There's no place like ... there's no place ...*

Finis.

She pushed him off and dressed quickly. She ran out of the apartment and into the street, gulping the air, gasping from the terror that pinched her shoulders. When she arrived home she bathed and tried to drown her singing skin.

She lifts her head up out of the water. New tears falling. Her own. Shame.

The bath water is cold.

The body begins to reject the soul for its yearning. This is aging. After leaving Barbados for the last time, Simon came to think of home as a yearning fulfilled only by love, which transformed yearning to belonging. When he met Faye—tall, fair, with frightened eyes—he felt full, complete and without cavernous reverberation. He was home in her strength and softness, contradictions like the soul of a bird. His skin began to tighten; excitement rushed blood to all his organs. Does the soul confuse the body when it loves, making love a mansion, tricking sagging skin to tightened, erect sensation?

But then love and home abandoned him again for almost a year. He moved out and lived in a colleague's basement, working long hours and watching endless hours of television at night, not calling and not calling Faye. Perhaps it's why he feels so at home here in this basement. For months he couldn't feel his toes in winter. He gained weight on a diet of pasta. His hair greyed, strand by strand, into silver wires. He tried not to think. No one knew how to reach him; he had disappeared underground. But one day it was too much.

And now, now . . . forgiveness gnaws like corroding salt, itching, begging to enter my pores. I scratch, I scratch . . .

Faye pulls the plug and the drain gulps down the soiled, oily water. She gets up and dries herself, slips into her nightgown. She can hear Simon in the kitchen again. Another drink. He has taken off *Figaro* and Nina Simone skates onto the CD player . . . *wild is the wind, so wild is the wind . . . you touch me, I hear the sound of mandolins, you kiss me, with your kiss my life begins . . .*

By the time she got home from David's Faye already felt severed from Simon, and when he came in from work the wrinkled shirt and tie he wore caused her even more panic. She went to him and undid his tie, smoothed his hair, and ran her fingers over his tired face. She struggled to seduce him, to have the wild wind blow them both away again. She made her advances but he was too tired.

Opera is silly, stilted and forced, mythological, with the absence of concrete things, like earth or wind. I love Nina Simone because she sounds unloved, screaming from somewhere deep below flesh: " . . . give me more than one caress, satisfy this hungriness . . ."

When Simon came back to Canada and fell in love with Faye, everything was easy. Even his job at the meat-packing plant didn't bother him. They would make love just looking at each other. Every moment was taut, stretched like a rubber band to its maximum elasticity; one inch further and he would've snapped to a pleasure from which he would not have been able to recover. Faye had music that he'd previously been deaf to, and he abandoned himself, for the first time ever, in waves and waves of the unknown, as though he had never left the surf that day the birds first came . . . . *he'd trade the world for the good thing he's got . . . when a man loves . . .*

He'd had nothing to prove anymore. He was snug. After the initial euphoria, though, sometimes his confidence would waver; a fear that he was not enough of a man for her would rise to the surface. She was so sophisticated, so smart, so beautiful, a beauty lost even to herself. *Why did she love me?* He tried to provide for her so that she could concentrate on her music. But in the early years she refused to play, said she'd lost her desire, lost her touch, was afraid of music. Over the years of her silence he started to forget that she had once been a musician.

Perhaps love is just about the thing itself—subject and object—love as the perfect reflection of itself.

David wanted to see her again. He called her office repeatedly, and she would speak softly and say no, no, no, no, to everything he said, every drop of nourishment he offered—*no, no, no* . . . in any language, *no*.

Then, abruptly, he stopped calling, and in the following month she learned from Simon that David and Justine had been having problems, and that David had moved and was staying at a friend's apartment.

In the meantime, Faye kept up the daily calls, dialling numbers, trying to sell opera, dance, or concert subscriptions. Sometimes when the work was slow she did other jobs, conducting surveys to find out what people were watching, what phone companies they were using, what running shoes they were wearing. The numbers came at her like families of seven, configured with different faces, eyes, noses, but together tapping out a code to someone, a voice, then a whole chain of other lives—existence in sevens.

The next time David called, he was prepared. He said simply: "singin' bodies don' forget," into the phone and then was silent, just breathing, wishing, hoping with all his might. Maybe on the other end of the line he was clicking together his heels. His silence forced her to speak to him, to ask him how he was. Then he trapped her. He asked her to meet him, just one more time, to call him at the apartment where he was staying, and meet to clear it up between them, to close what they had opened, to forget, to forget. She agreed, with part of her brain knowing the truth, the other part on automatic pilot. She wrote down the telephone number, memorized it, then tore up the slip of paper.

She concocted a story, one in which she was going out of town for the night to see Mary, who had moved to Sutton on the shore of Lake Simcoe. Even as she told him that Mary's husband was away on business and that her friend was in the city for the day to see a specialist and to shop, Faye knew she should stop the charade, but something propelled her on. She made Simon dinner and watched him eat with fatigue. Her head and body battled each other. Simon kissed her goodbye affectionately, saying he'd miss her. Her heart, trapped in her skin's lie, couldn't turn back. Leaving him Mary's number was passed over. They were supposedly meeting downtown, so she took the subway to Yonge Street and got out to call. She dialled seven digits from memory and didn't wait for hello:

"Where will we meet?" she asked quickly, breathless, and wanting to go home.

There was static silence.

"David? David?" She heard breathing, then repeated, "David? David?"

Then Simon's voice answered: "Faye . . . I don't understand."

She hung up. Her chest turned to lead and pushed her body down. She collapsed to the ground in front of the phone booth.

She didn't go home right away, but sat drinking coffee in a small shop near the subway. When she finally had enough caffeine for courage, she took the subway back across the Viaduct and slowly walked the blocks to their home. In the fading light the house looked shabby, in need of paint. She'd never noticed how neglected the exterior of their home looked. Simon was in the basement, as he is now, not wanting to speak to her.

It was days before they spoke, and then only about the routine of their days. Finally she went to him as he sat at his desk one evening. He didn't look up. She started softly, trying to explain, trying to lie to him and to herself, that she had agreed to meet David out of concern for him and his family, because he'd needed someone to talk to, because he'd lost his spirit. Knowing only that her own reasons for agreeing to meet David had something to do with the music she wasn't playing, she told Simon that she was worried that David might lose his way entirely.

Simon knew the truth. He forced himself to see things differently, tried to understand, each time they talked. Slowly he did, and slowly he began to touch her again, and slowly, very slowly, they were coming back to love.

It was then that Simon surprised her with the tickets and the flowers. Two years have passed since Faye ran into her Paris concierge with the peacock eyes, two years since Béla Bartok brought her back to herself, back to music. Gentle, delicate contact resumed: touching, kissing on bridges over the Seine. But for Simon's flu, the vacation was a success. They had escaped the stale air of deception that had hung about their home. Paris was restorative and the wild wind blew through her again . . . *like a leaf clings to a tree, oh my darling cling to me, for we're creatures of the wind, and wild is the wind, so wild is the wind* . . .

When they returned home she sold her old cello and bought a better, more aged and mellow instrument, and she started to play again. Intense practising produced aching arms. She slept soundly for a few nights, but then it started. She'd wake up in the early morning with the room spinning, her guts tossing. She'd run down the hall and lurch to the bowl, wretching bile, then wracked by dry heaves. The first two nights she convinced herself it was the jet lag and the playing. But then a few more and, no, no, no . . .

Simon would come up behind her, stand in the doorway, and watch as she reversed herself into the porcelain. This continued for a week, until one day he just didn't come home.

Unlike Simon, Faye has never believed wholly in science. For her, all stories are part of a larger cosmic opera—science but a recitative within the narrative. She knew all the theories. Darwin's natural selection was tied to the cycle of population growth, which produced inevitable competition between similar creatures, such as two wild horses trying to escape the same predator. One wild horse is very much like another, but they are not identical; one does run faster and escapes, while the other is killed. But the Bible's prognosis is quite different, giving the race not to the swift nor the battle to the strong.

Pregnant after years and years of trying, she was carrying David's child. It was to this child, this collection of cells that magically formed to bring into existence a new creature, one that turned the lives of fully formed humans upside down, that the race belonged.

In the efforts to save endangered species, modern techniques are used to determine when wild females are in season. The animals can be brought down in their habitat, anaesthetised, and impregnated with the sperm of a captive male. Eggs from recently dead wild females can be rescued and matured, then fertilised *in vitro* and transferred to wombs of captive females. Reversals of natural selection, an evening out the battlefield.

Faye spent days in bed, getting up now and then to vomit and then crawling back to bed on her hands and knees. She dreamt about Simon: his kindred cells were swimming within her, battling her body, asking questions . . . *who? who? why? why?* . . . then, *barf, barf . . . . I don't know*. She made it to work just once, wanting and desperately not wanting the growing demon inside her . . . *Simon, oh Simon* . . . her insides turning out . . . but knowing someone would have to feed it. The battle continued. Body and heart in opposite corners . . . *where are you?* . . . until one day she vomited on her pillow and started to bleed. The delicate cells, tired of the physical and metaphysical war, detached themselves from her uterus. In hospital she slept, barely dreaming, seeing shapes in the windows or on the faces of friends. Wild shapes, like the monsters of childhood, appeared on doctors' glasses, on plates of glutinous food. At the end of the week everything went monochrome and silent. Nothing rattled. The nurses sent her home.

The house was huge, disordered, and echoed with her movements. The days continued without her. She went to work but wasn't present. She began to hear sounds she would associate with Simon. She'd hear his footsteps, his breathing beside her. Each morning she'd wake to the ringing of a telephone. Seven numbers, seven numbers—the seven simple numbers that could reconnect her the way they had severed her from him. She was sure he was phoning her, trying to come home. But shaking her head out of sleep she'd realise the ringing was from the inside, a stinging buzzing silence.

Mozart enjoyed deceit, but musical form still superseded the content of his operas. In a letter to his father requesting a new libretto he says: "The most essential thing is that on the whole the story should be really comic; and, if possible, he ought to introduce two equally good female parts, one of these to be *seria*, the other *mezzo carattere*, but both parts equal in importance and excellence. The third female character, however, may be entirely *buffa*, and so may all the male ones."

Faye wonders if Nannerl would have reversed those specifications with all-female buffa. Starring Faye, the grand prima donna buffa? Would content have preceded form? Was she in Nannerl's opera? All bumbling content and no smart, hermetic form?

Mozart's *Cosi fan tutte* is immersed in deceit . . . "*and thus do we all*," its only moral legacy. It's the story of a woman in love for the first time with a man who is her friend's lover, disguised as an Albanian nobleman . . . *tutti accusan le donne* . . . . *that's just they way things are* . . . *Cosi fan tutte*. . . *thus do we all*. It was an exclamation not in the original libretto, but added by Mozart himself, as though he, *diabolus ex machina*, was exposing our beautiful deceit and gauging our reaction from the vantage point of eternity.

Faye knew she would never be able to speak to Simon at work. She found out where he was staying—with a friend from the ministry—and called him there, tried to speak with him, to win him back. He agreed to see her, just once. *Thank you, thank you*. She planned the meeting carefully, choosing their favourite Greek restaurant on the Danforth, wearing the blue-and-white dress she knew he liked. When she sat before him she spoke softly, trying to melt him again. She was a court jester trying to win the smile of a king. She tried familiar gestures and jokes. The King did not laugh. Most of all she tried to explain, but even to herself that was impossible. He said very little during their brief meeting. Now and then his bottom lip would quiver; then he'd sip his drink. And then, finally, he said: "No." Just no, then no again, then no one last time. He got up and left. *Click, unplugged.*

He went back to his friend's basement. He didn't call. Weeks passed. Her heart wore out; it had no tricks left, and was giving out with the loss of every last memory she had of his touch. Simon had locked her out of his universe. She felt damned to autopsies of regret. The should-have-done's, the should-have-done's. *I should have wrapped my legs so tightly around him that he'd have been buried so deep that it would have been him that became my child, my future. I should have told him about the place behind my right ear, which, when kissed, became the truth. The truth was something I needed to have kissed into my skin, a thin spot behind my ear, a very thin spot, unlike the other spots that grew thick with fear. Kiss it again, kiss it again.*

should have done
should have done . . .

Simon sits at his desk, staring at the report. *Providing for myself and for Faye is more and more difficult every day in the small air-tight office on Queen's Park Crescent. I wear my tie dutifully.* The cartography division is a place in the present, a fleeting place that tries to keep up with change, but which will never produce anything of merit or anything that will last. It was born of paper, not of the necessity of earth, not of whispering limestone. It is sterile. *I catalogue maps, struggle with the accuracy of meridians and parallels and write reports, but, even so, nothing is living in me. The present has disappeared.*

Faye walks to the bedroom, which is in darkness, and prepares to perform the trick, the game she used to play after Simon had left. She holds out her hands in front of her and walks into the room. Only a vague light from the alley, which filters through the heavy curtains, allows for the hint of silent forms in the room.

A large bed: weary covers were bunched together to one side, the bed no longer made in the mornings. All sense of order gone. She'd stretch her arms out in front of her, seeking a brush with something . . . *the beating of wings?* She'd walk slowly toward the bed, trying to be quiet so as not to wake him, anticipating her own surprise at finding him lying there. She'd be convinced by anxious blood in her palms that the pulse she was hearing was his breathing, that all of what had happened had been something she'd read or dreamed and that he'd be there when her fingers finally found the lamp beside the bed. She'd hold her breath. Twisting the switch like a flint between her thumb and forefinger, she'd see a cold light slap the wall. The bed was empty. She'd crawl, shivering, under the knotted sheets that could have been his body.

One night, a month into Simon's absence, a tingle began at her right temple as she lay on the couch. The pinpricks turned to a throbbing. It was as if she had slept too long on the side of her face, and blood was now rushing back to the skin. When she woke in the night her brain was boiling. The pain was excruciating and blisters had bubbled to the surface of her skin. There was a patch under her right eye puffed up like a leper's sore; another rash boiled under her right nostril; yet another over her eyebrow. She stayed awake, waiting for the morning to make them disappear, but by dawn there were more itchy patches, the pain was more intense, and her face had swollen to a boxer's mug.

She took the subway to the doctor's office downtown, sitting demurely at the back of the car. A man approached and looked at her sympathetically as he sat down. She felt reassured that the disfigurement was not as severe as she had thought. Another man did the same, but this one began telling her how beautiful she was and asked her to come with him to his place. She got up and moved unsteadily to the other end of the car. Yet another smiled and winked. It dawned on her that she was wearing the brittle aphrodisiac of a different sort. She looked as if she had been beaten, and these men wanted to console her, or contribute, she wasn't sure which. That landscape frightened her. She hurried off the subway at the next stop and took a taxi to the medical building.

The doctor told her she had shingles, *rosenblatten* in German, for the belt of blistering roses, as they usually occur around the waist, and in English named after their resemblance to the layered, slated tiles on roofs. Adult chicken pox. A herpetic virus that attacked a healthy body at its weakest moment. For three weeks she suffered with headaches and blistering pockets of flesh. She wore an eye patch to hide the rosebud eruptions that forced her eye shut, and to ward off predators when she travelled to work. When the blisters healed, she kept the eye patch pinned beside her bathroom mirror. The only sign of the shingles now is a scar under her eye. But for a slight discoloration of the skin, it is smooth and flat like the lie it represents.

Simon has never noticed, or at least noted, its presence. As he leaned over his brother's coffin and pressed his finger to the long larval ridge burrowed across David's cheek, Faye rubbed the mark beneath her own eye.

David and Faye . . . and me in a basement, forever underground . . . is it possible to resurface? The space between bone and flesh seems to widen, collapsing again in death: home at last. Life is an accident. Shouldn't love be the only thing that produces life? Love, like a god giving life, rendering the gift of childhood, that magical moment when sea birds bear messages of hope and fancy, signalling a path for the soul . . .

The floor creaks as Faye returns to the studio. She cradles her cello and stares into the sound hole, gazing back into her loneliness without Simon. The month turned into two, then three. Winter came and more months passed. She found herself in a routine, trying to regain strength. She went to work, and in the afternoons would take long walks along the lake to wear herself out, to wear out time, at first hoping that Simon's anger would abate and he would just come home. But in the dreariness of February she gave up all hope of his return, so she would walk just to reach time's logical end. She dug into never-before-explored parts of herself as a way to rip off calendar days that blew across the water.

Her cello listened and responded. She practised again, new pieces and old, reforming muscles, her fingers more dextrous than ever. Her hand and arms would throb in the darkness, waking her, and she'd writhe about in bed for hours before falling back to sleep. But the pain didn't stop her. She continued her conversation with the hollowed wood torso, rubbing it, torturing it with the bow. It learned to empathise with her.

The shingles had reduced her energy, and she couldn't regain the weight she'd lost. Circles shadowed her green eyes. She could feel her age. In the spring she started to take vitamins and tentatively began to work out—jogging, sit-ups, push-ups—anything to stay out of her head. Cooking complicated meals that involved hours of preparation became her passion. She'd fancifully decorate dinner plates with sprigs of herbs or wild flowers. She'd chill bottles of Chardonnay or Chinon and drink wine with the meals served to herself in the tiny dining room. Her routine was precise, deliberate; she immersed herself in acts of physical confirmation. Gradually she grew to enjoy her solitude. She wondered if she was learning to be alone as a way to learn to die.

Standing in front of the bathroom mirror one Saturday morning, her thin stare told her she should visit her father. In her sweater, tights, and heavy wool coat, she took the subway to Islington and then a bus to her father's apartment building. They sat together in his grimy living room and spoke only occasionally. He would make comments over the blaring television about items in the news and then later about the characters in a sixties sitcom rerun. Faye made tea for him and started to clean up dishes in the kitchen while he watched the show. She wondered then if her father had ever visited her mother's grave, and realised that she had no idea what truth her parents might have shared.

She tried to remember her mother, to drag her out of the foul sounds and the frightening last moments of her life, her ditty to clean dinnerware, and to remember what she'd been like when Faye was a child. She couldn't place her. The only feelings that surfaced were pity and regret at not having had long enough with her, not being adult enough to have known the tempo of her mother's sorrow during all those days and nights of her nagging rhythm of dissatisfaction. Against the television's canned laughter, Faye was struck with the knowledge that what her mother had given her was that tempo. Without previously acknowledging it, she had known her mother more deeply than she had ever wanted to admit. Tears loomed. She fought them, holding on to the strides she had made in banishing the metaphysical, remaining in the physical so as not to lose control. Then she let go, but it wasn't frightening. The sounds didn't come. They didn't take over. She sat down beside her father and dared the sounds to overpower her the way they had her mother. But she remained calm and stable. She knew then she'd be fine. She had transformed her mother's mad ditties into the arpeggios on her cello. As she got up to say goodbye to her father, Faye accepted the noises in her head, the only voice she had of her mother—a souvenir.

Outside in the street, tears came. These tears were not for her mother but for her motherhood, the wild horse that galloped away with all her love. She cried then, in silence, only a furrowed brow giving her away. She hailed a taxi and went home.

Her routine continued until the summer. She was content, planning to look for a roommate in the fall, perhaps a student, to help fill the spaces of the house and to pay the bills that were piling up. One day, the phone rang as she was cleaning the toilet, her hand deep in the bowl wiping hard under the lower rim as she tried to finish up before answering. The ringing continued determinedly. She reached the phone breathless, "Hello?"

"Me here."

Simon. The physical short-circuited, and Faye was plugged back into the universe through his voice. "Wondering how things are . . ."

"Things . . . (How could she speak about things to him? They did not exist in the world of things.) . . . are going along."

She tried to hold on to her new self, to honesty. She tried to match his, but she was in territory grown unfamiliar and her steps uncertain. When she finally gained the courage to ask him to meet, he agreed. She held on some more. At the café near their house, he spoke in monosyllables and looked worn and bloated; he was losing his battle with the present. She asked him to come home, and he said *where*. Our house, she said, and he didn't answer. It hadn't been a question. But he followed her out of the café. By the time they walked the few blocks to the house he looked worse, his face pale and eyes watery. He said he'd stay, just for awhile, just to see. She knew that this was the greatest act of love anyone had ever shown her. He had agreed to peel back the rind of trust to see what ripened beneath.

He was distant, silent most of the time, but he loved her, she knew that. *He loves me still.* He moved back in and they have been advancing and retreating for this last year, touching only occasionally. They've talked of trying to make a child and have made love on two timed and deliberate occasions—trying to cement the future. Now David's death has forced something new.

She breathes into the sound hole again, hearing her breath, then her voice echoing . . .

Is love as strong as death?
Is love as strong as death?
Is love as strong . . . ?
Is love . . . ?

They have seven years between them. Seven: the number of charity, grace, and the holy spirit. Early writers saw it as a number of completion and perfection. When the friends of Job came to comfort him, they sat down with him upon the ground for seven days and nights. Jacob, as a sign of perfect submission, bowed seven times before his brother. Seven joys and seven sorrows of the Virgin. *Is this the day of Judgement?* There were seven angels bringing seven plagues, which are the last, for with them God's wrath is completely expressed . . . but also, absurdly: seven dwarfs.

The earth was made—perfection—and then on the seventh day, God rested.

Is love as strong as death?

Faye sits in her studio, remembering, just as Simon sits in the basement, even as she wishes for the gift of amnesia, a gentle erasing of time. Just a synaptic nudge into nothingness and the pleasure of forgetfulness. Forgetting is easy, it's memory that stings like a perfect word, or note, or touch (the singing of bodies). Memory sits on the tongue, heavy and thirsty, and tasting of the stale and bitter crumbs of history; forgetting is a lithe dancer in abandon, pronouncing only a pulse, touching only the air—

listen:

in the downbeat,

though,

a distant ache.

CHAPTER 7

Tears

Simon's sister, Maggie, is a doctor. After studying in England for many years, her accent is curvaceous, with Bajan leaping over and widening the Bristolian, with Bristol puckering under wide Caribbean *e*'s, tightening them when she tries. The accent tattles on her for straying from the island, but nothing could have kept her from returning to Barbados to open a practice and be close to her mother and father, who now depend on her.

His abdominal muscles strain and fail on the twenty-second sit up, and Simon falls back to the floor to rest, just a beat. He is warm now, sweating slightly; he begins again . . . *23, 24.*

Perhaps it is because England is an island like Barbados, only wetter and colder, that it was possible for Maggie to return. For David and Simon it had been impossible to go back for good after the expanse of North America, where everything is so vast, so new and running rampant. Only nature ran rampant in Barbados; nothing else could compete.

. . . *25 . . . 26 . . . 27 . . .*

Maggie is defiant in her own way. She is the most independent of the four children, having refused the notion of marriage, even with several offers from lovers on both islands. She remains single, singular, and, Simon believes, still secretly in love with the gardener, Best, as though once she loved the best nothing else would ever do. But that leaves her free for her father's doting. Her degree in medicine is his reward for having left Guyana—the proof of his good judgement.

. . . *31 . . . 32 . . . 33 . . .*

At the funeral parlour, Edwin clutched Maggie's arm as if she were hope itself. Before the service began, he asked her to lead him over to the coffin. Simon saw his trembling fingers reach out to touch David's right hand, which cupped his left over his abdomen. Simon could almost feel the touch himself— a brush between charged and inert flesh that conceded to the mockery of existence.

. . . *34, 35, 36* . . . Simon is trying to make it to sixty sit- ups a day.

He wonders if Edwin secretly gambles at the track—for the hope. Phillip told him that Edwin and Grace have been having wild arguments, Grace accusing Edwin of attending the track not to treat the horses but to bet on them, risking their hard- earned savings. Phillip was scant on details, but he told Simon of MacKenzie's mumbling about the wages of sin and of Edwin's mood swings. Perhaps Edwin now sees everything as chance: the luck of breeding, the luck of livestock, the luck of birth, the risk of place. Over the last few days Edwin and Grace have been at different points in every room, out of sync in time and habit: the distance that hope travels to disappointment, that birth travels towards death—a torn-up road.

As the pallbearers lifted David past the mourners down the stairs of the chapel, Simon, gripping his assigned handle, glanced over to see MacKenzie's knees buckle slightly. She was wearing a borrowed wool dress and wool coat for the Canadian autumn. The sleeves rode up her arms, exposing fat wrists, and she pulled down regularly on the cuffs as though trying to keep her balance. Simon thought of her discomfort and longed for a glimpse of her shift. MacKenzie has softened with age; still evangelical, but not fearful. Her hair has turned silver at the temples, shining like lamps to the beyond.

MacKenzie never approved of David's or Simon's move to North America. Here, she said, "de devil found his garden . . . all dem freedom and selfishness—nottin' to care about 'cept yaself . . . dat's why de people does smack each udda up, does mek war in dey own backyard. Dey don' care about dey own people, only demselves." When the news about David reached the family, she begged Edwin to bring her to Toronto for the funeral, saying that she needed to see "Masta David," as she still called him, for herself. To shake her fist at the devil that had taken her boy, by showing up on the soil of his garden and vowing that the devil had not won yet.

. . . 57, 58, 59, 60!

He stands up and touches his toes. He twists his waist to the left *. . . ahhh . . .* to the right *. . . mm, mm . . . mm . . .*

MacKenzie now lives with the Carters and keeps watch over Maggie, Francie, and her brood. Phillip drops his family off at Willowdale each morning before heading to the Continental Hotel, where he manages the staff. Francie needs much help with her two children and is grateful for MacKenzie's firm hand. Clayton—Cal for short—is the older of the boys. He has inherited his father's circus spirit and is always playing tricks on everyone in the Garden. When he's not allowed to watch television or play the video games he loves so much he makes mischief in the neighbourhood, leaving knotted hoses on front steps, which then erupt in the hands of the unwary. He climbs the breadfruit trees and hides from his mother, who wanders about worriedly calling "Clayton! Clayton! . . . ya come here right now," while he giggles silently above her. Francie looks lost in the corporeality that has assaulted through her children. Simon wonders if she still reads romance novels. Where does she escape to?

Grace remained strong, firm in her steps, and unflinching through music, verse, and sermon. She greeted the guests stoically, as though she was there to comfort them in their sadness and loss, not the reverse. At the end of the service she stood at the coffin, smoothing the pillow, touching David, wiping his brow, as all mothers do to all children: a gentle but firm rub, a sacrament of sweat into skin, mother touch, mother hope. She summoned tranquillity to guide her, even while her desire surged over the satin of the coffin to hold her son. Her reaction shamed Simon's own salt-wind sadness, his stiff bones inquiring again and again as he gripped the coffin's handle: *And me . . . And me?* Simon was consoled by the sight of Grace lifting her foot to her calf in a gesture he knows so well. Her curtsy to grief. And, as though darning a tiny hole in fabric even after a garment has become unwearable, Grace reached for Faye's hand and held it to her chest as she moved aside to let the pallbearers through.

All through the service, Phillip stood sullenly at the back of the chapel, wearing dark glasses. He moved from one side to the other, a pacing panther between pews, then stood still to watch while the rest prayed. Each time Simon looked up, Phillip would peep over his sunglasses and stare right at him, as if wanting to say something, or to holler it, finally, with all the dozing wrath of his race. Simon would turn back to the prayer or to gaze around the chapel at the young cousins sitting together, who looked everything like each other and nothing at all. Five of them: David's three girls, Rita, Miriam, and Vanessa, and Phillip's two boys, Clayton and Edwin Jr. Rita is tan-skinned, with a slim, serious face like Justine. Miriam has her mother's fair skin, but is round and squat like Francie. Vanessa— sweet Vanessa, the youngest—looks exactly like David. Mendel's wrinkled pea. Clayton and Edwin Jr. both settle in at brown, with matching eyes. Simon looked at the wide-eyed gaze of the five children and wanted to be in those eyes. Not in view, but inside their vision, with hope and future still unclouded. He surveyed their tiny bodies, legs dangling in the front pew. The pelicans dived; he tasted salt, licked his lips, was inside a wave headed toward a shore. He stared at Vanessa, who always seems out of place, detached, dangerously unwanted in a way that shows in her swinging legs, more self-conscious, more aware of the distance to the ground. She is the one who most resembles the Carters, yet seems the farthest away from a moment in Guyana where skins were marked and graded, where brooms swept out the unwanted and empty cups starved warring tribes. She too, Simon notes, was born in a year of the dragon. *She smiles very little—poor little bird, poor tender leaf . . .*

He holds his breath and bends to touch his toes.

Faye stares at herself in the mirror. She pulls out a grey hair from a patch near her ear. She examines her mouth. Puckers to thicken her lips. She turns to her profile and wrinkles her button nose.

In the Mediterranean there dwells a sea worm that has an extraordinarily long nose—three to eight inches long—while its body is the size of a peanut. It's this magical nose that distinguishes it, along with the fact that only females have a separate, physical existence from their mothers. The catheter nose searches for larvae that have been left by other female worms in the seaweed. It sniffs out appropriate candidates for ingestion. Those she doesn't swallow remain in the seaweed to eventually hatch and become more females. Those she swallows become male and live the rest of their lives inside her peanut-sized torso, acting as in-house sperm donors that she uses to fertilise her eggs. Breeding is simple for some females.

I am ovulating today, I can feel it.

Children are goosebumps on eternity. Touch them and the moment demands something of you, some sort of recognition of excitement, terror, or astonishment. A hair standing at attention, cells alert and over-stimulated: a promise. *What would have been Sean's promise to me? An inherited ability from Michael to unplug me, to block me out with the turn of his head? And David's child? This day? Would his promise have been this same sorrow? What's in store for David's children?*

Perhaps children only fool us—the trick of life. Hope. Children, parents, lovers, all consumed by each other as a way to escape from ourselves. *And this is love?* But children are our mirrors, leading us back to ourselves, calling attention to our weakness: our snivelling need to be more than what we were born.

A few years ago, Faye ran into Michael on the street. She trembled through the whole meeting so casually come across, yet so dreaded for years. He smiled at her affectionately, and seemed genuinely happy. Faye invited him for a coffee. They talked the way they always had, avoiding some topics, connecting where connection had always been the strongest. Michael was calmer, less concerned with himself, more vulnerable, like she'd always wanted him to be. He talked of travel, of health and exercise. He was married to a writer; they had two children. Softer, yes, less compelling . . . more like . . . Faye. He had filled up his distant parts with bits of her, and she was living inside him. She wondered how many one-way conversations he'd ended with her words, how many tears he'd shed at seeing movies that would make her weep. She recognised love's gift: there are parts of everyone we've ever loved inside us. Becoming them, we become the world.

"What to do with freedom?" David asked him the last time they saw each other.

Freedom, freedom, freedom, Simon repeats as he sweeps up the pine dust from the floor of his work space. *Freedom, freedom . . .* He stoops to draw the broom to meet the dustpan, which he then empties into a garbage bag. He shuffles to his desk and sits down. He drains the last of the rum from his glass.

The question had been rhetorical, but David had held his brother's gaze expectantly. Simon turned away. They were sitting in the kitchen on a Sunday, just over two years ago, sharing a drink, talking about nothing in particular, and clocking the deep fraternal pauses that had always separated them. David had just moved out of the house he shared with Justine and the girls, but told his brother only that their problems were "sore, sore." Inevitably the conversation turned to family. They spoke about their father, about the way he had never forgiven David for choosing music and not university. Talk of Edwin had sent David into the past—to his first days in New York.

Arriving in America had felt like arriving at an accident, he said to Simon. It was like happening upon a tragedy of life, not knowing what had caused it or how anything would ever be the same again.

"They only know what's black and white—no room for brown." In America, David became a Negro, Afro-American, black, and wore an afro to prove it to anyone who didn't know where he fit. "Not black, not white, no choice," he said. He'd played with a few bands, but at that time the island music he wrote was popular only among expatriates like himself, and it had been the islands he had been trying to escape—their confines, their slowness, the inferiority complex bred in the bone.

"If you're black in America, there's only one place to look, and every time ya look there ya see a mountain of bones—slave bones—same as home. But there they tell ya to be free. And freedom is for those who're pure. But they don' admit it . . . and ya only get purity from breedin'."

Then he paused, grinned as usual, adding: "An' breedin' backfires 'pon you anyhow."

He rambled on after that, blurring the past and present, New York and Toronto.

"Sometimes it just means to knock down the guy who gets in your way. Free to make the most money . . .

"This man who ran a bar in New York, he asked me to sell things for him . . . told me he was goin' to be rich, but I just saw him slavin' and making me a slave too . . . to buy things, sell things ... mountains of bones pilin' high high so." He gestured with his arm raised above his head. "*Born in the USA, I was born ...*" The words of the song tumbled out. "People don' want art, they want the artist—or to be him or to kill him, whichever; it's not about what he makes, just about who he is ... cause they could be him if they wanted ... or so they wish ... *Aahh, how does it feel ... how does it feel ... to be on your own, like a complete unknown ... like a rollin' stone ...*"

Simon watched and listened in fascination, seeing his brother converge with MacKenzie and her country bush wisdom.

David was no longer the sharp wild boy whose voice had stung Simon to the quick that day at the lighthouse, but a rounded middle-aged man, with thinning hair, a falling, unhappy face.

"They tell you you can have what you dream. Mostly we get what we always had ... sometimes we get vulgar ... *they say everything can be replaced, they say every distance is not near ... so I remember every face, of every man who put me here. I see my light come shining ... from the west down to the east ... any day now, any day now ... I shall be released ...*"

Then he stopped and gazed straight ahead. A long silence ensued. Simon fidgeted. David looked at him.

"You know, that girl, Kelly, the one in Kingston ... I never did, you know ... never ... made her do it. She wanted it ... bad, but I couldn't ... man, I couldn't do it ... couldn't ... perform, you know ... get it up. I was too frightened. She got mad as shite at my being limp, started screamin' ... and then she said that."

A flood of relief burst forth from Simon's lungs. It was the explanation he had hoped for, to replace the words that had stanched the flow of his past. He felt a tear sliding down his nose. He shifted, got up from the table to pour some tea.

"So, these last couple of weeks must've been hard. You

getting to see the girls?" David only stared hopefully at his brother. The lump in Simon's throat vaulted.

David gave Simon a gift that day: an antique compass he'd found in a store. Simon rubs the smooth brass case of the instrument. He takes it from his pocket and opens the case, lays the compass gently on the desk examining the fine script etching of *N.S.E.W.* before him. All possible paths. David had never bought him anything, and Simon had not understood the gift when it was given. After opening the box, he had felt a strange shudder of confusion. "Oh," he said, then put it on the kitchen table, slid out of his chair, said, "I'll be right back," and went to the basement. He sat at his desk blankly and didn't return for over an hour. When he went back upstairs, David was gone; the compass was on the table. It was the last time Simon saw his brother alive.

Faye turns from the mirror and starts to clean up the studio that she's littered with scraps of her life—photos, letters, diaries. She tidies, throwing some things away.

Suicide is fastidious, often preceded by meticulous arrangement of details, the appointment of belongings, making order for those who are left in chaos. What were David's last actions just before he killed himself?

When David left Barbados, he left its size. Everything about it was size, he'd told Faye. Small, small, small, except for the ocean that surrounded it. He wanted hugeness, space, freedom. And people with poetry leaving their lips when they swore. In New York he had felt music expand and fill his life. But when day to day survival settled in and forced him to find ingenious ways of keeping his small room on Clinton Street, things changed. Faye knows very little of the story of what happened to him when he first came to Canada to see Simon in Kingston, but she knows he got into some kind of trouble there. "Sometimes everythin' just bash up in ya face, and it's like you payin' for all ya ever did." In Toronto he started to earn his living playing music. Then came Justine, the three children, then Faye.

Justine never found out about Faye. David's separation from Justine had not been about unfaithfulness but about David's vacuumed spirit and the tensions over financial problems. Justine moved back to Newmarket to the nest of family willing to help out with the girls. He was left alone in Toronto, "widout my three babies, my three lambs." He pulled himself together, working his shifts at the jail to pay all the bills. Faye ran into him downtown, some time after Simon came back to her. They ordered coffee in a café and he talked to her with his eyes groping the horizon behind her.

"You can't fuck your way to yourself . . ."

"Meaning?" she threw back sarcastically.

"I mean, fucking is about wanting someone to tek hold of you and point you back in your own direction, but it doesn't work."

He sipped his coffee. "And duplicating yaself doesn't help eitha. You know from the time I was eighteen I'd have sex with any woman who would have me." Faye's stomach churned. "Dogs," he said, "don' know how to stop eatin', and I was a stinkin' starvin' mutt. But I've never loved anyone like Justine. Never had so much calm."

David ran a hand over his then closely cropped hair. "I've applied for a job at the corrections facility in Newmarket. It's better pay, and it'll mean I can be closer to my girls. At some point, feeling chained is the right thing."

Faye heard from Justine three months later that David had got the job at the Newmarket jail. Soon after, he was promoted. He started to make a life there, to see Justine as often as possible. He saw the girls regularly. Newmarket became his home, the place he wanted to settle. He would raise his lambs there, he told his mother, raise them to be strong and smart. He got involved in the community, for their sake, going to parent-teacher meetings with Justine, taking the girls skating at the arena. Respect, respect.

Faye has been to Newmarket three times: once a few days ago, today, and once when she was a teenager with friends going to a summer party. At that time it was a motorcycle town, tough and trashy, but, slowly over the last twenty years, it has become a bedroom community—a booming place to where disgruntled suburbanites have fled Toronto to escape encroaching immigrant neighbours. Immigrants fleeing immigrants. She doesn't understand David there. Chained, he had said . . . the right thing . . . *chain, chain, chain* . . . *chain of fools* . . . It mocks the pain of imagining him there.

David worked hard for the next few months, but as the recession deepened, he was given fewer shifts. He drove a taxi at night. Debts piled up. Depression came, his own, which he shared with no one, except Justine, and only when she would drop her guard and ask. He started to acquire things he couldn't afford. He put on a brilliant show of burgeoning affluence, buying a car phone, a big-screen TV. He joined a fitness club. He made new friends he hoped would share their influence. The Newmarket police chief, who recognised a public relations opportunity, invited David to join the Rotary Club. David accepted . . . *respect, respect* . . . to fit in, finally, to secure his place in the community.

David was invited to the annual Rotary Challenge before being accepted into the club. His initiation included having to answer questions about his job and the penal system.

"Cite the seven orders listed in the Code of Discipline pertaining to a correctional worker's relationship with offenders," demanded the designated Rotarian.

David stood up to answer. He managed the first three

effortlessly: no maltreatment, harassment, or abuse; no improper use of authority; no personal or business relationships. He paused and considered the rest. No exchange of gifts or favours. No contraband. But then he got flustered at the attention and confused the last two points. He stuttered out something about written permission to hire an offender, which was correct but with which he resigned himself to failure and sat down, shaking his head with an embarrassed grin. The club-house antics proceeded and he was forced to pay a symbolic fine for his so-called crime by having to sit out the rest of the ceremonies behind jail bars made of cardboard. Humiliation. The police chief, his sponsor, played along. Later, David told Justine that, more than the personal failure, he had disappointed his sponsor. Justine had paid no attention to his exaggerated disappointment. She told Faye the story only a couple of days ago, saying she thought that event was the beginning. *The ending*, as Faye now knows.

The next day, David phoned the police chief to apologise for his bungle at the club challenge. The secretary, after requesting his name, put him on hold, then came back to him, saying that the chief wasn't able to speak to him. David took this as a personal rejection, a punishment for failure. In fact, Faye discovered today, the chief had left work early that after-noon and his secretary told everyone that he wasn't available.

Mozart is laughing . . . *cosi fan tutte* . . . and thus do we all.

The following week passed in depression and withdrawal not seen before by Justine. David was ill-tempered with her; he made unscheduled visits to see the girls, against her wishes. He made three appointments with the bank to discuss a loan, all of which he failed to keep. He called his insurance company. He mailed off rubber cheques for overdue bills. One night he called almost everyone he knew "just to chat." He called Simon and

Faye, but got only the answering machine. He called his parents in Barbados to, as Grace put it, say a hello.

The next afternoon after work, when a fellow guard dropped by for a visit, David was leaving his apartment. He locked the door but gave his friend the key. The friend asked him where he was going. All David said was, "for cigarettes." He didn't come back.

According to stories pieced together over the last few days, David's behaviour had continued to be erratic and contradictory, right up to the end. He called his friend from his car on the highway, leaving a message, telling him that his car had broken down near a deserted barn on a country road north of Newmarket. Then, apparently, David had gone to the barn equipped with a suitable rope and attached it to a wide beam in the loft. From a series of marks on his neck the coroner believes that he failed in his first attempt. Faye pictures his face above her. *There's no place* . . . The coroner supposes that he grew flustered, desperate. He called Justine, but couldn't reach her, and left a similar message on her answering machine about his car breaking down. He returned to the barn. This time he was successful. Justine found him dangling from the loft, sunlight slashing his clothes through the slats of old barnboard.

And Simon's face today: a mask. Faye has no idea of his feelings or what the pattern of his thoughts was. He was merely present, as though able to pour out a glass of himself for others to taste. He filled his body like water fills any container to its shape. He watched and helped, studied others' faces but didn't give into the despair in them. He was able to keep them separate from his own spirit, the fluid of Simon.

I can't stand the music on the cd player any longer: Yo Yo Ma—Japanese Melodies—making the cello whine. I was enjoying Nina Simone. Why did he change it? Perhaps he put this on for me, but it's not what I want, not now. I'll slip in Marvin Gaye softly . . . what's goin' on? . . . .

The compass points Simon back to the cemetery, to David's coffin.

Clouds began to break apart as the limousines and cars pulled up to the burial plot in Newmarket's Highland Gardens Memorial Cemetery. The sun loomed behind an edge of grey cumulus, tinting everything metallic. In this modern cemetery, simple bronze plaques in the grass mark the grave with the name of the deceased and dates of birth and death. As Simon grabbed the handle once again, to lift the coffin from the hearse, he could see Vanessa playing in the mound of dirt that had been dug to make room for her father in the earth. Her hair is like his sister Maggie's, longer and darker brown; the curls blow about the top of her head despite an elastic band that tries hopelessly to contain them.

No one else had seen her drift over to the mound. No one else was watching her, as she patted and sorted the dirt, measuring out portions for an imaginary guest who was either to eat her offering or hoard it, it wasn't clear which. She was getting seriously dirty, but remained engrossed in her play with the invisible friend. Simon's legs wobbled for a second and he lost his pace, feeling a shifting inside the coffin, the box tilting toward his side. He looked up, and the other pallbearers—David's two friends and three other jail guards—caught his eye accusingly. He straightened, gripping the handle harder. The wind picked up. Faye finally pulled little Vanessa from the mound and took her over to stand by her sisters and mother beside the limousine. Faye combed Vanessa's curls and tried to clean off her dress, grooming her like a cat would a kitten.

Simon spins the compass and it swirls on the desk. Marvin Gaye is crying softly on the stereo . . . *I want you, in the right way.*

I want you, but I want you to want me too, just like I want you, whewew . . .

Cemeteries are sculpture gardens where the dead have sprouted marble as art for the living. Faye believes they should be extravagant, generous, solid expressions of grief and passing, not the modernist minimalism of Highland Gardens where David lies beneath a small rectangular plaque the size of a postcard. Paris's Père Lachaise is the kind of place where she'd like to be buried. Monuments to achievement, to art, to grief that cracks and crumbles through time, while roots of trees press up stone, and vines grow like the dead's fingernails. There, perhaps, the dead converse in the middle of the night, speaking of history, piecing together their errors, correcting the tragedies of their time. Molière and Marx chatting near a mausoleum. Collette and Jim Morrison flirting on a newly filled mound. Does blood have more meaning there, where who you were born still means how you will live, how you will die? Her ancestors came here to escape the confines of their birth, but was being equal a trade-off for splendour?

Her mother lies under a small headstone, her name inscribed modestly on the marble. It's simple but prominent, at least it stands up out of the earth so that walking through the cemetery at night one might trip on the stone, forcing someone to remember her, if only in a curse.

Faye puts the photo of her mother, father, and brother at Niagara Falls back into the box of old letters. She closes the closet door. She loosens her bow and places it with the cello in their case. Each move is deliberate and careful. In the last few days, she has had to concentrate on order.

In the two days following David's suicide, the chaos of disbelief prevailed; someone had to take control, to wade through the questions and sort out the pieces of David's last days. She accompanied Justine to his apartment. It was tidy, stacks of bill receipts, statements, and policies arranged in neat piles on the kitchen table. He was looking after everyone. Each member of his family had been left a note in separately sealed envelopes, and on each envelope was the directive not to open it until he had been buried. When Faye gave Justine hers, she tore it open immediately and then broke into wailing. Faye gathered up the envelopes and guided Justine out of the apartment.

She hasn't given Simon his note yet. *I fear it so desperately, so fully, as though it will finally break us.* It is the envelope that is in the hallway chest. She hid it there as soon as she returned from David's. But perhaps it is time that it was opened. *I will open it for him; I must know. I will go down again . . .*

As the dirt was thrown onto David's coffin and the minister spoke of ashes and dust, Simon tried to see Mackenzie's face. Was she singing the song about walking through a storm? MacKenzie believes in salvation, even though her god is always threatening vengeance and punishment.

"Saul was a great king, anointed by de Lord, but sometimes de evil spirit would visit he and torment and trouble he . . . and for dat he needed music, and was David who played sweet sweet 'pon he lyre and soothed de soul of de king wid he sweet music . . . But David, too, he didn't trust . . . naw, he was afraid of many tings, even of Saul. He went to de land of the Philistines and fought 'dem Philistines and slaughtered all a dem at once. De Lord made him King, and, you know, David was a man, he made mistakes like any man, and God punish' he, but always when David ask his forgiveness, he forgave he and David lived a long life . . . until he got cold, couldn't stay warm . . . and died."

MacKenzie repeated this story over and over in the days after their David left Barbados. After the burial, while the mourners made their way to the cars parked along the lane, MacKenzie remained hugging Simon's mother, rubbing her back, while Grace bent over the grave, weeping quietly. Edwin, Maggie, Phillip, Francie, and the children waited beside the limousine. MacKenzie bent to lift Grace from her knees. Her voice was as forgiving as rain: ". . . as far as de east is from de west, so far has He removed our transgressions from us." Grace stood and allowed herself to be guided toward the limousine by MacKenzie. She kept her eyes to the ground, but MacKenzie looked up and toward the horizon and continued gently, in the softest voice Simon had ever heard her use:

"As a father loves and pities his children, so de lord loves and pities those who fear him, for he knows our frame . . . we are dust . . . our days are as grass . . . mercy and loving-kindness of the Lord are from everlasting to everlasting . . . His righteousness is to his children's children . . ."

Simon swallows hard, then again, to stop the lump in his throat from vaulting again.

Perhaps to have a child is my salvation—to give most what I need most—a return to a moment by the sea, the glory of that moment before knowledge. He fears that MacKenzie has touched him to the core after all. Where is the governing principle of the present? Could it be that the most human of activities—science and its raw materials, hypotheses—spring from an emotional, not rational source? The same source as the rush of fire in David's voice? Will the DNA trail lead us to sweat, to inspiration, to doubt? What did Mendel mean when he whispered to his student: "*Meine Zeit wird schon kommen*," *my time will surely come?* He left his research to become Abbot of Brunn. Was he or was he not referring to the future of the science of genetics and the process of unification?

There are pieces of Simon all over the basement. He wants to refasten himself, to make love to Faye to see if the birds will dive again.

It is almost dawn. If the morning catches him here in the basement the tears will surely come. But he's not tired. He has two choices—to begin again or to join his brother in the slowly freezing ground. To begin again . . . alone? With Faye? Making a third? Can he stay?

Trust. Trust is a path. Trust is rock. Trust is what ancient stone has for humanity—to allow itself to be blown apart by a stick of dynamite wedged in a crevice, so that a human road may forge a path deeper into the future, leaving parts of itself along the side of the road. Sliced, exposed particles of shy granite.

Am I strong enough? I will go upstairs. Perhaps we will talk. What does she want? The rum has softened my knees.

Faye stands in the hallway, her feet anxious on the wooden floor. A thin draft from under the door next to the oak chest eddys around her ankles. She holds the small padded envelope addressed to Simon in David's hand. It's thick, clearly containing something more than paper. With her thumb she pushes down on the padding; it's mostly air, but her fingers feel a delicate outline. *Is this the corner of death I must tear open?*

Something springs out as her as she tears away the glued flap. It's straw. A fat reed from a broom. And a short note:

> A journey is possible
> only if you remember what you've left.
> Forgive me.
> I love you,
> David

My god, is it all so simple?

He approaches Faye, who stands motionless at the far end of the living room. She stares out the window as brown, curled leaves blow past the house. Her shoulders are curved, heavy. Her arms hang straight at her sides.

A few tentative steps, but he hears the scrape of his own footfalls and doesn't want to startle her. He pauses, not knowing how to proceed, and sees something in her hand. A piece of paper and . . . a pencil? . . . no, too long . . .

Light is creeping into the trees. *Ahhhahh, mercy mercy me, things ain't what they used to be . . . . where have all the blue skies gone . . .* the music plays softly. She sees a fat squirrel scurry along the grass with something in its mouth. It scales a tree, disappears into the golden leaves.

He must touch me or I will cleave . . . cleave to . . . cleave from . . . the same word with two different meanings . . .

Simon stands still by the front door. He focuses on the straw. He takes another step and the hardwood creeks. Faye turns around. His eyes are strained on the golden object in her hand. She steps toward him.

I must give this to him . . . Here . . . forgive me too . . . Touch me . . . .

He looks up at her face, into those frightened-animal eyes. *Do I do that to her?* She holds up the straw, stained like litmus paper, with the blood that tests them.

After death, the blood in the body dries to powder akin to the chalky blush of women's makeup—just as temporary and fragile. The stain on that straw marks activity, wetness, the flow of cells, the passage of life through matter. She holds it so tentatively, trembling. He takes another step. *Did he give it to her? . . . David . . .*

She steps. The squeak of the floor is loud, too loud. She steps sideways onto the rug so that her movement is silenced. She looks down, but holds out the envelope and straw as she goes toward him. Her eyes move up as far as his hands, to the pictures in his palms, the lines like rivulets in the earth, gutters carved in mud by a storm.

The song is repeating itself . . . *ahh, ahh, mercy mercy me* . . . He doesn't know how to react to her holding out the straw—to take it? How did she get it? He is loose, and falling away. He is suddenly fatigued, more tired than in all his life. His hands stay limp at his sides.

If he kisses me I will know the truth . . .

❧

What is the content of mercy?

❧

He looks like a ghost. Is love stronger than death?

❧

We have the same sagging skin, the same echoing distance from bone. How can you kiss yourself and not dissolve? Can we be? . . .

❧

I hold out my hand . . . take it . . .

❧

Hands . . .

❧

A child . . . .

❧

Mercy.